Obscure

Pasado Futuro

Copyright Page

Obscure
© 2024 Antonio Perez, writing as Pasado Futuro
All rights reserved.

ISBN: 979-8-218-56716-3

Cover Design: Mark Baiz

Published by Antonio Perez, writing as Pasado Futuro
Orlando, FL, USA

Printed in the United States of America

For permissions, inquiries, or additional information, contact:
Antonio.Perez.V@outlook.com

Table of Contents

Dedication

This book is for my friends, my family, and all those who have made a positive difference in my life.

Though not everyone may be mentioned by name, please know that your impact has given me the courage and confidence to share my story with the world.

My goal in writing this is to reach and inspire just one person. Anything beyond that is a blessing and a beautiful bonus.

Thank you for being part of my journey.

Prologue

Navigating a world marked by ignorance is no easy feat, but it's the world I've always known. I am a member of multiple minority groups, which often places me in spaces where I feel like an outsider looking in. Both my Puerto Rican and Italian heritage have given me a rich, diverse cultural foundation, but they have also compounded the sense of not truly belonging anywhere. To some, I'm too "ethnic"; to others, I'm not enough. It's a balancing act between conflicting identities that I've been forced to manage since I was young. Adding another layer to this complex reality, I identify as a member of the LGBTQ+ community. This has given me yet another badge that simultaneously makes me proud and isolates me.

My life's journey has been about seeking a sense of acceptance while refusing to hide any part of myself. This book is my attempt to share that journey with you, to offer you a glimpse into the life of a man who has constantly grappled with fitting into spaces that were never truly designed for him. These are the moments and experiences that have shaped me, my insights, my opinions, and the lessons I've gathered along the way.

This book is structured as a series of short stories, arranged in chronological order. These stories are more than just glimpses into my past; they are pieces of a larger puzzle that, when assembled, show the journey of a boy into manhood, a man who continues to struggle and grow. By sharing these experiences, I hope to reach others who may feel as I have—like they don't quite fit in, like the world around them doesn't always make sense, or like they're being asked to pick a single piece of themselves and ignore the rest. I understand what it feels like to navigate a world that can feel suffocating, full of labels and expectations.

In my own way, I want to offer you the assurance that you are not alone. No matter where you come from, or who you love, or how you identify, there is always a way forward, always a way to build a life that embraces your truest self. I want this book to be a reminder that, no matter how different or misunderstood you may feel, there's value in sharing your story. You never know who might be waiting to hear it or who might be encouraged by it. By tastefully sharing our struggles and triumphs, we have the power to make a positive impact on others and to help them find their own path through the chaos of life.

Life isn't easy. We face hurdles, we get knocked down, and we question everything. But in those moments, it's important to remember that there's strength in vulnerability, and that sharing our stories can transform them from personal burdens into sources of collective strength. I hope you find solace, hope, or even a little piece of yourself within these pages. Thank you for joining me on this journey, for taking a walk through my memories, my mistakes, and my victories. This is the story of my life, and I hope, in some way, it resonates with yours.

Wolf

The first day of freshman year was overwhelming. I stood just outside the entrance, taking in the waves of students streaming into the building. Some were chatting excitedly, clearly friends already, while others looked just as lost as I felt. I shifted my backpack higher on my shoulders and took a deep breath. This was a new start—a chance to meet new people, to reinvent myself if I wanted to.

As I walked through the crowded halls, I could feel my stomach twist with nervousness. High school seemed like an entirely different universe from middle school, and the size of it alone was intimidating. I glanced at the crumpled map in my hand, trying to locate my first class, but it felt like every hallway looked the same. It didn't help that I kept brushing shoulders with people who seemed to know exactly where they were going.

Lunchtime came faster than I expected, but I was relieved. At least I'd get a break from finding classes and hearing teachers repeat rules and expectations. I grabbed a tray of food, scanning the cafeteria for an empty spot. That's when I heard someone call out, "Hey! You looking for a place to sit?"

I turned around and saw a tall guy waving me over. He had brown eyes that seemed to light up with mischief, and his grin was infectious. Next to him stood another boy, a bit shorter but with a confident stance. The two of them looked like they'd been friends forever, and they were already laughing as I approached.

"I'm Ian," the tall one said, reaching out a hand to shake mine. "And this is Joey."

Joey gave me a nod and a half-smile, which was made even more noticeable by his braces. He had a slight muscular build and a serious expression, but there was a playful glint in his eyes.

"I'm glad I found you guys," I replied, relieved to not be sitting alone. "First day, and I'm already feeling like a fish out of water."

Ian chuckled. "You and everybody else. Don't worry, we'll show you the ropes."

Over the next few days, lunch became my favorite part of the day. Ian and Joey were the kind of friends I hadn't even realized I'd been missing. Ian was a goofball—he had this deep voice that could command attention in an instant, but he mostly used it to crack jokes and make the people around him laugh. Joey, on the other hand, was a bit more serious, almost the yin to Ian's yang. He could be goofy, sure, but there was a calmness about him that made you feel like he had things figured out, even if he was only a freshman like the rest of us.

We'd sit together, huddled over trays of school cafeteria food, sharing ridiculous stories and planning our next big pranks. Ian was always coming up with these crazy ideas, like filling lockers with balloons or sneaking into the school after hours to hide fake spiders in the teachers' lounge. Joey would listen with an amused smirk, sometimes rolling his eyes, but I could tell he enjoyed the thrill of it all just as much as Ian did.

One afternoon, Joey leaned in, lowering his voice like he was about to share some deep secret. "Hey, have you heard about YDC?"

I shook my head, curious. "No, what's that?"

Ian's face lit up. "Oh, man. It's this volunteer organization we're part of. Youth Directors Council, or YDC for short. It's under the Police Athletic League—ever heard of it?"

I nodded slowly, piecing it together. I'd heard of the Police Athletic League, sure, but I'd never really understood what it was all about.

"So, it's like a program to keep kids out of trouble," Joey explained. "They do all sorts of community stuff—park clean-ups, car washes, that kind of thing. The whole idea is to keep kids in parks, not prisons."

"Yeah," Ian added, nodding enthusiastically. "And the best part? They have this annual conference. We just got back, and it's insane. You get to listen to motivational speakers in the morning, and then in the afternoon, they take you to a theme park. It's the coolest thing ever."

I could feel my interest growing with every word they said. Here was this chance to get involved in something bigger than just school, something that felt real and important. I could sense a thrill in their voices, an excitement that I rarely saw at school, and it made me want to be a part of it.

"You should come with us to a meeting," Ian said, his tone almost daring me. "It's open to anyone who wants to join. And trust me, it's a lot more fun than it sounds."

The following week, Ian and Joey were buzzing with stories from the conference, recounting the speakers they'd heard and the crazy rides they'd been on. They made the whole thing sound magical, like an experience that was far removed from the routine of school and homework. They must have noticed how hooked I was because, by the end of lunch, Joey looked at me and said, "Seriously, you have to come to the next meeting."

I hesitated, thinking about how my mom would react. She was always so protective, barely letting me go anywhere that wasn't school-related. But the thought of being a part of something like YDC was too tempting to resist. I went home that day, rehearsing what I'd say to her, trying to figure out the best way to convince her to let me go.

The more Ian and Joey talked about YDC, the more intrigued I became. I'd always imagined myself getting involved in something outside of school, but I never knew exactly what. Listening to their stories about the conference, I could almost picture myself there sitting in a room with hundreds of other teens, feeling the energy of motivational speakers, and then letting loose at a theme park afterward. It sounded like a dream come true.

One day during lunch, I finally worked up the courage to ask them how I could get involved.

"So, how does someone join YDC?" I asked, trying to sound casual even though my heart was racing. "Do I just show up at a meeting, or is there more to it?"

Ian grinned. "It's easy. The meetings are open to anyone. We meet every other Saturday at the community center. Just come with us next time, and you'll see what it's all about."

Joey chimed in, nodding. "You'll love it. It's a good way to meet people, and it feels good to be doing something for the community, you know?"

Their enthusiasm was contagious. I knew that I had to be there. Now, I just had to convince my mom.

At home, I rehearsed my pitch, trying to anticipate every question my mom might throw at me. She'd always been overprotective, and I knew she'd have reservations. But this felt important to me—maybe even a little life-changing. I found her in the kitchen, chopping vegetables for dinner, and I launched into my carefully prepared speech.

"Mom, there's this program I'd like to join," I began, trying to sound as confident as possible. "It's called the Youth Directors Council. They do community service projects and events, and it's all about keeping kids involved and out of trouble. Ian and Joey are part of it, and they really think it'd be a good fit for me."

She looked up, raising an eyebrow. "And what exactly would you be doing?"

I explained everything I knew about YDC—the park clean-ups, the car washes, the chance to attend events and conferences. I emphasized how it was part of the Police Athletic League, hoping that the association with law enforcement might reassure her. I could see her weighing it all in her mind, her eyes narrowing as she considered the pros and cons.

"Will there be adults supervising?" she finally asked, her tone cautious.

"Yeah, of course," I replied, a bit too quickly. "There's a whole council of adults who oversee everything. And it's all in safe, public places."

She sighed, setting down the knife. "Okay. But I want to meet Ian and Joey. And if I ever find out you're not where you're supposed to be, you're done."

I grinned, relief flooding through me. "You got it. I promise."

When Saturday finally arrived, I was buzzing with excitement. Ian and Joey met me outside the community center, and together we walked into a room filled with kids of all ages. The energy was infectious—everyone seemed to be talking at once, and there was this sense of purpose in the air that I hadn't felt before.

The meeting kicked off with a brief introduction from Mrs. Brimer, one of the adult coordinators, who explained the agenda for the day. She talked about upcoming projects, including a park clean-up and a fundraising car wash. As she spoke, I felt a surge of pride knowing I was about to be part of something that was bigger than just me. This wasn't just about hanging out with friends or killing time; it was about making a real difference.

As the meeting wrapped up, the YDC secretary, a girl named Jenny, approached me. She was maybe a year or two older than me, with a no-nonsense expression and a clipboard in hand.

"Hey," she said, glancing up from her notes. "I heard you're new here. We're looking for someone to lead the park clean-up next month. Interested?"

I was caught off guard. I hadn't expected to be given any responsibility on my first day, let alone something as important as leading an event. But the way she looked at me, like she already believed I could do it, gave me a strange boost of confidence.

"Yeah," I replied, trying to keep the excitement out of my voice. "I'd love to help."

Jenny nodded, scribbling something on her clipboard. "Great. I'll send you the details, and we'll set up a time to go over everything. Welcome to YDC."

Over the next few days, I threw myself into planning the park clean-up. I spent hours researching how to organize volunteers, contacting local businesses for donations, and making lists of all the supplies we'd need. It was my first taste of real-world responsibility, and I found that I actually enjoyed it. It was as if a whole new side of me was coming to life—a side that wanted to take charge, to make things happen.

I spent a lot of time talking to Ian and Joey about the project, and they helped me out wherever they could. We'd meet after school to brainstorm ideas, and sometimes they'd come over to my house to help me make flyers or plan out the logistics. The three of us had this unspoken agreement to back each other up, and it felt good to know I wasn't alone in this.

As I walked into the community center that day for the park clean-up meeting, I was still trying to familiarize myself with all the faces. Some were recognizable from the previous meetings, but there were always new people joining, making it a bit challenging to keep track of everyone. Despite this, one person caught my eye almost immediately, a constant in every gathering I'd attended so far. He seemed to radiate energy—Carlos.

Carlos was already deeply ingrained in the YDC, that much was clear. He had this natural charisma, the kind of presence that made him seem larger than life. He was tall and lean, with dark hair cropped close and glasses that framed his expressive eyes. I noticed that he often made others laugh, drawing people in effortlessly. I envied his ease, the way he seemed so sure of himself, so comfortable in his own skin.

On that particular day, he was at the center of a small group, discussing the logistics of the upcoming park clean-up. I listened from a distance, impressed by the way he spoke. He had this genuine enthusiasm, a passion that was contagious. He wasn't just ticking off a checklist; he was getting everyone excited about picking up trash. It was like he could turn the most mundane task into an adventure. I found myself gravitating toward his group, wanting to be part of whatever he was talking about, just to soak up some of that energy.

After a while, Carlos caught me watching and shot me a smile. My heart skipped a beat, and I quickly looked away, feeling a little embarrassed. I wasn't used to being noticed. But then, out of nowhere, he walked over to me, extending his hand with that easy grin of his.

"Hey, I'm Carlos," he said. His voice was warm, inviting.

"Nice to meet you. I'm Pasado," I replied, shaking his hand and hoping he didn't notice the slight tremble in my fingers.

"I've seen you around," he said, tilting his head slightly. "You're new, right?"

"Yeah, just joined a few weeks ago," I replied, trying to sound casual.

He nodded, his smile never faltering. "Well, welcome to the chaos. It's nice to have new faces around. Are you enjoying it so far?"

"Yeah, it's great. I like the sense of purpose here, you know?" I replied, trying to match his easy demeanor. "Feels good to be doing something that actually makes a difference."

"Totally. That's why I joined too. It's like, for once, we get to decide what we want to change," he said, looking out at the room of people. "Plus, it's a cool way to meet people."

There was something in the way he said that last part, a glint in his eye that made me feel like he was talking about more than just casual friendships. I felt a blush rising in my cheeks, but I managed to hold his gaze, curious and intrigued.

From that moment on, Carlos and I seemed to find each other at every meeting. I learned that he'd been with the YDC for over a year and that he was passionate about giving back to the community. He told me stories about past events, everything from organizing car washes to hosting fundraisers. His enthusiasm was infectious, and I found myself looking forward to our conversations, craving that connection.

One afternoon, after we'd wrapped up a particularly grueling park clean-up, Carlos and I lingered behind, chatting as we gathered supplies. He started telling me about his family, about his upbringing, and the challenges he faced growing up in a neighborhood not too different from mine. I listened intently, soaking in every word, finding similarities in our experiences that made me feel understood on a level I hadn't expected.

And then, he turned the conversation toward me.

"What about you? What's your story?" he asked, leaning back against a tree, his gaze fixed on me with genuine interest.

For a moment, I hesitated. I wasn't used to people asking about my life, about what made me tick. But there was something about Carlos that made me want to open up, to let him in. So, I did. I told him about my strict upbringing, my protective mother, and how joining YDC felt like a breath of fresh air. I even mentioned how nerve-wracking it had been to step out of my comfort zone, to try something new.

He listened without interrupting, nodding occasionally, his eyes never leaving mine. When I finished, he gave me a soft smile, one that felt like a reassurance.

"Sounds like you've been through a lot," he said, his voice gentle. "But hey, you're here now. And from what I can see, you're doing a damn good job."

His words settled over me like a warm blanket, filling me with a sense of belonging I hadn't felt in a long time. Carlos had a way of making me feel seen, of making me feel like I mattered. It was a feeling I was quickly becoming addicted to, even if I wasn't entirely sure what it all meant.

After the success of the park clean-up, I felt a new sense of purpose. I hadn't just participated; I'd led. And for the first time, I felt like I belonged somewhere. I began attending more YDC meetings and volunteering for projects whenever I could. Ian, Joey, and I became regulars, and soon enough, we knew most of the kids by name.

The more I got involved, the more I noticed how everyone in YDC was there for their own reasons. Some were like me—newcomers just looking for a way to get out of the house and do something worthwhile. Others had been around for years, and YDC was a second home to them. But regardless of our backgrounds, we all shared this unspoken understanding. We were here because we wanted to make a difference, and because, somewhere along the way, we'd found a community that welcomed us.

Carlos was quickly becoming one of the main reasons I looked forward to each meeting. We seemed to end up on the same projects more often than not, and I found myself growing more comfortable around him with each passing day.

One Saturday afternoon, we were volunteering at a car wash fundraiser. The whole thing was Ian's idea, and he'd managed to convince half the team to wear ridiculous costumes to draw in customers. Carlos and I were assigned to drying cars after they came through the wash, and we quickly fell into an easy rhythm.

As we worked, we talked about everything from our favorite bands to our worst fears. I noticed the way he laughed, this full-bodied, genuine laugh that seemed to come straight from his heart. I liked the way he'd brush his hair back when he was deep in thought or how he'd lean in just a little bit closer when he was really interested in what I had to say.

At one point, while we were drying off a particularly muddy truck, he glanced over at me with that contagious grin of his. "You know, I wasn't sure about this whole YDC thing at first," he admitted, wiping his hands on a towel. "But I'm glad I stuck with it. I don't think I'd be having half as much fun without you."

I felt my cheeks heat up, and I quickly looked away, pretending to focus on a stubborn mud stain. "Yeah, same here. I mean, I'm glad you're around. Makes things more interesting."

We fell into a comfortable silence, both of us smiling as we finished up the truck. It was moments like these that I started to realize that maybe, just maybe, I was feeling something more than friendship. But the idea scared me—I'd never felt this way about anyone before, let alone a guy. It was new territory, and I wasn't sure how to navigate it.

Over the next few weeks, Carlos and I grew closer. We started hanging out outside of YDC meetings, spending afternoons at the park, or just walking around the neighborhood, talking about anything and everything. It felt natural, easy. I found myself looking forward to our time together, counting down the days until I could see him again.

It wasn't long before I started feeling a pull towards him, something deeper than friendship, though I couldn't quite put it into words. I'd catch myself glancing at him, noticing the way the sunlight danced off his hair, or how his laugh seemed to fill the air, making everything around us feel lighter. I didn't fully understand what I was feeling, but I knew that being around Carlos made me happy, made me feel alive in a way that nothing else did.

One evening, as we sat on a park bench watching the sunset, Carlos turned to me, a thoughtful look on his face.

"You ever feel like you don't quite fit in anywhere?" he asked, his voice barely above a whisper.

I nodded, feeling a lump form in my throat. "Yeah. All the time."

He smiled, reaching out to place a comforting hand on my shoulder. "Me too. But being here, with you, it makes me feel like maybe I'm exactly where I'm supposed to be."

In that moment, sitting there with Carlos as the sun dipped below the horizon, I realized that I wasn't alone. We were two people from different worlds, yet we'd found each other, and somehow, that made everything make sense. I didn't know what the future held, but I knew that, with Carlos by my side, I was ready to face whatever came next.

One Saturday afternoon, Carlos invited me over to watch a movie. We picked an old action flick, the kind with cheesy one-liners and over-the-top stunts. As we sat on his couch, munching on popcorn and laughing at the ridiculous dialogue, I felt a strange warmth spreading through me. It was like the world outside had faded away, leaving just the two of us in this little bubble.

Halfway through the movie, Carlos shifted closer to me, and I could feel the warmth of his arm against mine. I glanced over at him, and our eyes met. In that moment, I felt a surge of emotion—something I couldn't quite name, but that felt both exhilarating and terrifying at the same time.

Without thinking, I leaned in, and he did the same. Our lips met, and for a brief moment, everything else disappeared. It was just us, sharing this quiet, intimate moment that felt like the start of something I'd been searching for all along.

When we pulled away, Carlos looked at me with a soft smile. "I've been wanting to do that for a while," he admitted, his cheeks turning a shade pinker.

I couldn't help but laugh, feeling a mixture of relief and happiness. "Me too."

As the days went on, our connection continued to grow. I found myself looking forward to our moments together, whether we were at YDC meetings or just hanging out after school. There was a sense of ease between us that felt natural, like we'd known each other for much longer than just a few months.

I also began to understand more about myself in ways I hadn't before. Being with Carlos made me realize that my feelings didn't fit neatly into the boxes I'd always assumed they would. I started to see that love and connection could take many forms, and that sometimes the people we're meant to be with aren't the ones we expect.

But as much as I cherished my time with Carlos, I also knew that our relationship was something I had to keep to myself. I wasn't ready to share it with the world—not yet. It felt too new, too delicate, like something that might disappear if I spoke it aloud. So we kept our moments private, sharing secret smiles across the room at YDC meetings and stealing quiet moments whenever we could.

The longer I stayed with YDC, the more I felt like I was part of something meaningful. We organized more events, each one leaving me with a deeper sense of accomplishment. I loved the way we came together as a team, each of us contributing in our own way to make things happen. And I found myself growing closer not just to Ian, Joey, and Carlos, but to everyone in YDC. They were becoming like a second family to me, and the community we'd built felt like a refuge.

As the weeks turned into months, I began to see the impact our work had on the community. We cleaned up parks, raised money for local charities, and hosted events that brought people together. It was more than I'd ever imagined when I'd first walked into that meeting. YDC was changing me, helping me grow in ways I hadn't anticipated, and I was grateful for every moment of it.

Carlos became a constant presence in my life, his laughter and warmth becoming things I looked forward to every day. He showed me a world beyond my own, a world where I could be myself and feel accepted. And in turn, I felt like I was discovering parts of myself that had always been there, just waiting for someone to bring them to the surface.

As my connection with Carlos deepened, I found myself caught in a whirlwind of emotions. I was elated and terrified at the same time. Each day spent with him felt like a new adventure, yet there was also an undercurrent of anxiety. I had never been in a relationship before—let alone with another guy—and I was still figuring out what all of this meant for me.

I had come to terms with my feelings for Carlos, but I was unsure how to navigate the world around me. High school was complicated enough without the added layer of having a crush on my best friend. I started to wonder what would happen if my feelings became public. What would my friends think? Would they support me, or would they turn away? It was a question that gnawed at me more than I cared to admit.

One day after school, as Carlos and I walked to the park, I decided it was time to voice my concerns. I had been feeling overwhelmed and needed to know where we stood.

"Hey, can we talk about something?" I asked, trying to keep my tone casual as we settled onto a bench overlooking the pond.

"Of course," he replied, his eyes bright with curiosity. "What's up?"

I took a deep breath, trying to steady my racing heart. "I've been thinking a lot about us—about what this is." I gestured between us, unsure of how to articulate my feelings without sounding foolish. "I mean, we've been spending a lot of time together, and I really like you. But I also don't know what that means for us."

Carlos nodded, his expression serious. "I've been thinking about it too. I really like you, too. But I get that it's complicated. We're still figuring out who we are, and the last thing I want is for this to make things weird between us."

His honesty was refreshing, but it also scared me. "Exactly. I don't want to lose what we have. But I can't ignore how I feel."

"Me neither," he replied softly, his gaze dropping to his hands. "Maybe we could just take things slow? See where this goes without putting a label on it?"

I felt a weight lift off my shoulders at his suggestion. "I can do that," I said, relieved. "Taking it slow sounds good."

We spent the rest of the afternoon talking about our hopes and dreams for the future, our fears about growing up, and the things that made us feel alive. But as the sun began to set, I couldn't shake the feeling that there was still so much more to figure out.

As the weeks passed, our relationship continued to flourish in secret. We shared stolen kisses and lingering glances at YDC meetings, always careful to keep our bond hidden from the rest of our friends. But even in our small bubble of happiness, I began to sense tension in the air.

It wasn't just my anxiety about being discovered. I noticed the dynamic among our group starting to shift. Ian and Joey were always supportive, but there were subtle moments when I caught Ian watching Carlos and me, a flicker of concern crossing his face. I could tell he sensed something was up, and that made me nervous.

One evening, after a particularly long meeting, I walked out with Ian and Joey. As we made our way to the parking lot, Ian fell back to walk beside me.

"Hey, I just wanted to check in," he said, his voice low. "You and Carlos seem...close lately. Everything good?"

I hesitated, unsure of how to respond. "Yeah, we're just hanging out more. You know how it is."

He gave me a knowing look. "You know you can talk to me, right? If there's something going on, I'm here for you."

"Thanks, Ian. I appreciate it," I replied, though I didn't know if I was ready to share everything with him just yet.

The tension came to a head one Friday evening during a YDC fundraiser. We were hosting a bake sale, and everyone was in high spirits, bustling around the community center with trays of cookies and brownies. Carlos and I were working together, but there was an undercurrent of unease between us. I could feel my anxiety rising with each passing minute.

During a lull in the action, I watched as Carlos interacted with the other volunteers, his laughter ringing out as he joked with Ian and Joey. It made my heart swell, but there was also a pang of jealousy. I wanted to be the one making him laugh, the one he focused on.

When he finally returned to my side, I felt a rush of frustration. "Can we talk for a minute?" I asked, my tone sharper than I intended.

"Sure," he replied, looking taken aback.

We stepped into a quieter corner of the center, away from the chatter. "What's going on with you? You're acting like everything is fine, but it's not. I feel like you're more comfortable with them than you are with me," I said, my words spilling out before I could stop them.

Carlos ran a hand through his hair, looking conflicted. "I didn't mean to give you that impression. I'm just trying to blend in and be part of the team."

"But I want to be part of your world too," I replied, the frustration bubbling over. "I don't want to feel like we're hiding. I don't want to be just your secret."

His expression softened, and he stepped closer. "You're not just a secret to me. You mean a lot, and I'm still figuring things out, okay? I didn't want to make things weird with the group."

I took a deep breath, trying to reign in my emotions. "I get it. But it hurts, Carlos. I want to share this part of me with them. With you."

Our conversation ended in silence, and we returned to the bake sale, the tension still thick in the air. I could feel the weight of my words lingering between us. Carlos tried to act normal, cracking jokes and engaging with the others, but I could sense his discomfort.

As the night wore on, I found myself increasingly withdrawn, wishing I could turn back time to when everything felt easy and uncomplicated. The event wrapped up, and as we packed up, I caught Ian's eye. He approached me, his expression serious.

"You okay?" he asked quietly.

"Not really," I admitted, feeling the urge to confide in him growing. "Carlos and I had a fight. I'm just worried about everything."

He nodded, understanding etched on his face. "Relationships can be tough, especially when you're still figuring things out. Just be honest with him. That's all you can do."

A few days later, Carlos texted me, asking to meet up after school. My stomach twisted with a mixture of anticipation and dread. I knew we needed to talk, and I wasn't sure how it would go.

When I arrived at our usual spot in the park, Carlos was already there, sitting on a bench and staring at the ground. He looked up as I approached, his expression unreadable.

"Hey," I said softly, taking a seat beside him.

"Hey," he replied, his voice low. There was a moment of silence before he spoke again. "I'm sorry about the other night. I didn't mean to make you feel like you weren't important to me."

I nodded, feeling a lump form in my throat. "I'm sorry too. I let my insecurities get the better of me. I just want to be able to be ourselves, you know? With everyone."

Carlos shifted, his gaze locking onto mine. "I want that too. But I'm scared. Scared of what people might think, scared of what it all means."

I took a deep breath, gathering my courage. "I can't promise it'll be easy, but I want to figure it out together. No more hiding."

His eyes softened, and I felt a surge of hope. "Okay. Together. Just know that I care about you, and I want to make this work."

We sat together in silence, the weight of our conversation hanging in the air, but this time it felt lighter. I reached out and took his hand, intertwining our fingers. It was a simple gesture, but it felt monumental—a step forward into the unknown together.

After that conversation, things began to shift. We started being more open about our relationship, even if it was just a small smile or a shared look during meetings. I could tell that Ian and Joey were starting to pick up on the changes between us, and surprisingly, I felt ready for it.

One day at a YDC meeting, as we discussed upcoming projects, Ian leaned over and whispered, "You two are adorable together." I felt my cheeks flush, but the warmth of his support was encouraging.

Later that week, we had a bigger project coming up—a community picnic that would involve the whole neighborhood. Carlos and I were tasked with coordinating activities, and as we brainstormed ideas, I felt a renewed sense of excitement. This was our chance to really show our commitment, not just to each other but to the community we were building with YDC.

We poured our hearts into planning, coming up with games, activities, and ways to involve the community. Each meeting felt like a celebration of not only our work but also our relationship, and the warmth between us grew stronger.

Carlos and I kept our relationship hidden from our families. As the months went by, the pressure of secrecy started to weigh on me. I knew that eventually, I'd have to confront my parents about my relationship and my sexuality, but the thought terrified me. For now, I just wanted to enjoy the connection we shared, free from judgment and expectations. Our bond felt fragile, like a secret world that only we could access.

Late one night, Carlos and I were texting from our respective houses. It was a weekday, and my parents had gone to bed hours ago. The only light in my room was from my phone screen, casting shadows on the walls. I glanced at the clock—2:15 a.m. Despite the hour, I felt wide awake, anticipation and nerves making my heart race.

"Do you want to meet up?" Carlos asked, his message tinged with excitement.

I hesitated. It was late, and sneaking out always carried a risk, but the idea of seeing him was more tempting than anything else. "Let's do it," I replied. "Where should we meet?"

Carlos suggested a small park about a mile away from both our houses. We figured it was secluded enough that we wouldn't run into anyone, especially at that hour. The plan was set: we'd meet at 2:30 a.m., giving us just enough time to slip away unnoticed.

I slipped on a hoodie, then cautiously opened my window, listening for any signs of movement from the rest of the house. Once I was sure no one was awake, I climbed out and dropped to the ground, making my way across the yard. The fence at the edge of our property was high, but adrenaline helped me over it. On the other side, I put on my rollerblades and set off towards the park.

The streets were eerily quiet, lit only by occasional streetlights. As I glided down the road, I felt a mix of freedom and nervousness. Just as I reached the end of my street, a car turned the corner. I recognized my neighbor behind the wheel—he was just getting home from his late shift. I held my breath as he drove past, hoping he wouldn't recognize me in the darkness.

Finally, I arrived at the park, where Carlos was waiting under the cover of a tree. Seeing him there, I felt a rush of relief and excitement. We shared a quiet laugh, the thrill of our secret rendezvous making everything feel surreal. We spent a while talking about everything and nothing, savoring each other's company until the sky began to lighten with the first hints of dawn.

I returned home just before sunrise, sneaking back into my room through the window. I was careful not to make any noise, but in my haste, I left my rollerblades outside. Exhausted, I fell into bed, still replaying the night in my mind as I drifted off to sleep.

The next evening, I was in my room playing video games when my parents barged in. My mom was holding my rollerblades, her face etched with suspicion.

"Why were these outside your window?" she demanded.

I froze, searching for an excuse. "I, uh, I went out for a bit," I stammered, avoiding her gaze.

My dad's expression darkened. "Your neighbor saw you rollerblading in the middle of the night. What were you really doing?"

They were looking for the truth, and I knew I couldn't lie forever. "I met up with Carlos," I admitted, trying to keep my voice steady. "We were just talking."

My mom's eyes narrowed, a flash of anger crossing her face. "You were sneaking out at night just to talk? Do you think we're stupid?"

My parents had a troubled past with substance abuse, and I could see where their thoughts were heading. My dad stepped closer, his tone growing harsh. "Were you out there smoking weed? Is that what this is about?"

"No!" I insisted, frustration rising within me. "It wasn't like that at all. We were just hanging out."

But the look in their eyes told me they didn't believe me. They exchanged a glance, and then my mom stormed out of the room, leaving me alone with my dad.

My dad's expression softened slightly, and he let out a heavy sigh. "Look, if there's something you're not telling us, now's the time. We just want to understand."

I felt like I was being pulled in a thousand different directions. Part of me wanted to keep the truth hidden, to maintain some semblance of control over my life. But the other part of me was tired—tired of lying, tired of pretending, tired of feeling like a stranger in my own home.

Tears filled my eyes as I took a deep breath. "Carlos and I... we're dating. I'm gay."

The words hung in the air, heavy and final. My dad's eyes widened, and for a moment, he just stared at me, speechless. Then he closed his eyes, rubbing his forehead as if trying to process what I had just said.

My dad left the room without another word, and for a moment, I felt an overwhelming sense of relief. But that relief was short-lived. The next morning, I woke up to find that my bedroom door had been removed, my TV was gone, and my window had been boarded up. It felt like a punishment, a silent but unmistakable message that things would never be the same.

My mom avoided me for the next three weeks. She barely acknowledged my presence, and when she did, it was with a cold, distant look that cut deeper than any words. I felt like an outsider in my own home, and every day was a painful reminder that I had shattered their expectations.

In the meantime, Carlos and I were both grounded. We were only allowed to leave the house for school and our sports programs, and even then, we had to come straight home afterward. Our relationship was put on hold, and the distance between us grew with each passing day. To cope, I started writing him letters, pouring out my thoughts and fears on paper. I missed him terribly, and those letters became my lifeline, a small reminder that I wasn't alone in this.

As the weeks dragged on, I found myself withdrawing further into myself. I spent hours lying on my bed, staring at the ceiling, replaying the events in my mind. My mom still wouldn't speak to me, and my dad seemed lost in his own thoughts, barely acknowledging my existence.

Eventually, my dad came into my room one evening. He sat on the edge of my bed, his expression a mixture of confusion and sadness. "Do you think you could still like girls?" he asked, his voice barely above a whisper.

I knew he was struggling to understand, and I wasn't sure how to answer. Part of me wanted to be honest, but another part of me wanted to appease him, to make things easier. "Yeah, I guess I'm bisexual," I replied, though deep down, I was still figuring it all out.

He nodded, and I could see a hint of relief in his eyes. But even as he left the room, I knew that things would never be the same. I had opened a door that could never be closed, and I wasn't sure if I was ready for what lay on the other side.

Word of my coming out somehow spread through my family. I began receiving texts and calls from relatives, offering words of support and encouragement. It should have been comforting, but instead, it left me feeling exposed. I suspected that my dad had shared the news, and the realization stung. He had broken my trust, and I couldn't shake the sense of betrayal that lingered in the air.

My mom, on the other hand, continued to keep her distance. She barely spoke to me, and when she did, her words were brief and clipped. I could feel the tension between us, an invisible barrier that grew thicker with each passing day. I had hoped that time would heal the wounds, but instead, it felt like we were drifting further apart.

When the grounding finally lifted, I couldn't wait to see Carlos. I counted down the days, longing to escape the confines of my house and feel some sense of normalcy again. My parents had begun to ease up, though the scars of the past few weeks lingered. I'd spent countless nights lying in bed, replaying our last conversation, wondering if things would ever go back to the way they were.

Carlos and I arranged to meet at a small café a few miles away from our neighborhood. I arrived early, nervously tapping my fingers on the table as I waited for him. When he finally walked in, a mixture of relief and anxiety washed over me. He looked the same as always—kind eyes, easy smile—but there was a distance in his gaze that hadn't been there before.

We greeted each other with a hug, though it felt more like an embrace between friends than the closeness we once shared. We talked about everything and nothing, catching up on school, sports, and YDC. It felt comforting to be with him, yet there was an undercurrent of tension, as though we were both avoiding the one topic that truly mattered.

After a while, he looked at me, his expression serious. "I've been thinking a lot, especially while we were grounded," he began. "About us, about everything that's happened."

My heart sank. I knew where this was heading, but I wasn't sure I was ready to hear it. "Yeah?" I replied, trying to keep my voice steady.

Carlos took a deep breath. "I think we should keep things... professional, you know? Just focus on YDC and being friends." His words were gentle, but they cut deep. He wasn't rejecting me outright, but the implication was clear: he wasn't sure if he wanted to continue our relationship.

I nodded, swallowing the lump in my throat. "I understand," I replied, though inside, I felt like my world was crumbling. I wanted to fight for what we had, to convince him that we could make it work, but I could see the resolve in his eyes. He had already made up his mind.

For the rest of our time together, we kept the conversation light, avoiding any further mention of our relationship. But as we said our goodbyes, I felt a pang of loss that I couldn't ignore. I knew that things would never be the same between us, and I wondered if I'd ever feel that same connection with anyone else.

As I adjusted to the idea of just being friends with Carlos, another challenge loomed on the horizon. At our next YDC meeting, I noticed him spending a lot of time with Kevin, a new member who had recently joined. Kevin was confident, outgoing, and charismatic—the kind of person who could command a room with ease. Watching them together stirred something within me, a bitter mixture of jealousy and insecurity that I struggled to keep in check.

Carlos and Kevin seemed to click instantly, sharing inside jokes and exchanging glances that felt all too familiar. I tried to ignore it, telling myself that they were just friends, but deep down, I knew that Carlos was moving on. It was a harsh realization, and it only intensified the feelings of loss that I had been trying to bury.

At first, I tried to keep my distance, avoiding Carlos and Kevin whenever possible. I threw myself into my responsibilities with YDC, hoping that staying busy would keep my mind off the situation. But no matter how hard I tried, I couldn't escape the nagging sense of inadequacy that followed me everywhere. I wondered if I had done something wrong, if there was something about me that wasn't enough.

The more I watched them together, the more I felt like an outsider in my own life. I had once been the one sharing those moments with Carlos, but now, it was as though I was invisible. I found myself questioning my worth, wondering if I had ever really mattered to him at all.

As the weeks passed, the sadness that had been simmering within me began to morph into something darker, something I couldn't shake. I found myself withdrawing from my friends, avoiding social gatherings, and spending more time alone. I would sit in my room for hours, staring at the walls, lost in a fog of despair that I couldn't seem to escape.

It was like a cloud of darkness had settled over me, suffocating and relentless. I knew that what I was feeling wasn't just sadness—it was something deeper, something that clung to me like a weight I couldn't shed. I tried to push through it, telling myself that I just needed time, but the emptiness only grew.

I started to lose interest in the things that had once brought me joy. My grades began to slip, and even my responsibilities with YDC felt like an overwhelming burden. I would show up to meetings, plastering on a fake smile and going through the motions, but inside, I felt hollow. It was as though I was living on autopilot, disconnected from the world around me.

I knew that I needed help, but I didn't know where to turn. My parents were still distant, and I didn't trust them enough to share what I was going through. The thought of opening up to them about my depression felt impossible, especially after everything that had happened. I didn't want to give them another reason to be disappointed in me.

In the quiet moments, when I was alone with my thoughts, the darkness seemed to close in, suffocating me with its weight. I would lie in bed at night, staring at the ceiling, feeling as though I was drowning in a sea of my own despair. The loneliness was unbearable, a constant reminder that I was alone in my struggles.

Suicide

Home life was a battlefield, each day bringing a new kind of war. My parents argued relentlessly, their voices a constant source of tension that filled our small house. My older sister, the one I looked up to, found herself at the center of this storm, bearing the brunt of my parents' frustrations. They believed discipline was necessary, a misguided notion that led to verbal and physical abuse. I could hear the anger in their voices, the strikes that followed, and the cries of my sister reverberating through the walls.

During those moments of chaos, my younger sister and I would retreat to our hiding spots, cramming ourselves into the cramped, dark space of the lower kitchen cabinets. We would huddle together, trembling, wishing we could shut out the world. The sound of our parents fighting was deafening, like a storm raging outside while we hid inside our fragile shelter. I could hear my little sister's quiet sobs, and I would place a finger to my lips, hoping to keep her quiet, praying for the storm to pass.

"Why do they have to fight?" my sister would whisper.

"I don't know," I replied, trying to sound brave. "But It'll be okay. Just stay quiet."

Our parents believed that tough love would straighten my sister out, but their methods were anything but loving. Wooden spoons, belts, and anything they could grab became tools of discipline. Each strike felt like a dagger in my heart, a reminder of the anger that loomed over us. I felt helpless, unable to stop the cycle of pain. I wished I could shield her from it all, but I was just a scared kid myself.

As the months dragged on, I felt the weight of depression settling over me like a heavy fog. It started slowly, creeping into my mind during quiet moments when I was left alone with my thoughts. The darkness wrapped around me, filling the void with despair. I smiled at school, determined to maintain my façade as a social butterfly, but it felt increasingly like a mask I wore to hide my pain.

"Hey, are you okay?" a classmate would ask, noticing my forced smile.

"Yeah, I'm fine," I'd reply, not wanting to burden anyone with my struggles.

But deep down, I was crumbling. My grades fluctuated, hovering around average, never quite reflecting my true potential. I wanted to focus in class, to drown out the noise of home, but the worries about my sister and the fear of what would happen next distracted me.

I took a part-time job at an Italian ice shop, a place filled with laughter and the sweet smell of sugary treats. It was my escape, a momentary relief from the chaos at home. Serving customers, making them smile, felt good. But when I returned home at night, the darkness would creep back in, reminding me of the struggles I couldn't escape.

Joining the after-school swim team was another attempt to find solace. I loved the water—the way it enveloped me, the freedom it offered. For those few moments in the pool, I felt weightless, as if I could float away from my problems. But even that relief was fleeting; the struggles of home life loomed like a dark cloud over my head, always waiting for me to resurface.

Then there was Carlos. He became a bright spot in my life, someone who understood my struggles and shared in my burdens. We would run into each other at YDC meetings and swim meets, exchanging glances that spoke volumes. But our relationship felt burdened by the pressures of my home life. I could see the shadows creeping in on both of us, threatening to extinguish the light that we found in each other.

As the pressures mounted, my thoughts turned darker. I felt like I was teetering on the edge of an abyss, and I feared that I might tumble in at any moment. There were nights when I wished for the pain to stop, for an escape from this life that felt so heavy. I began to harm myself, seeking relief from the emotional turmoil through physical pain. Each cut felt like a release, a momentary distraction from the chaos within.

Driving with my parents became torturous. The thought of jumping out of the moving car would flash through my mind, a terrifying escape plan that felt oddly appealing. I tried to drown the darkness in our pool one night, but the instinct to breathe always won. I would surface, gasping for air, even when the water felt like it could take away my pain.

The turning point came one day in school when we were assigned to meet with our guidance counselor, Ms. Crook. As I walked into her office, I felt a mixture of anxiety and desperation. The moment I stepped inside, I sensed a shift in the air; it felt like a safe space.

"Hi there! I'm Ms. Crook. How are you doing today?" she asked, her tone warm and inviting.

"I'm okay, I guess," I replied, trying to keep my voice steady.

"Just okay? I'm here to listen if you want to talk about anything," she encouraged, her smile reassuring.

I took a deep breath, feeling the weight of my words pressing against my chest. "It's just... things at home are really hard. My parents fight all the time, and my sister... she gets in trouble a lot."

"Fighting can be really stressful. How does that make you feel?" Ms. Crook asked gently.

"It makes me scared," I admitted, my voice barely above a whisper. "And I feel like I have to hide from it all."

"Have you talked to anyone about how you're feeling?" she probed further.

"No, not really. I don't want to burden anyone," I replied, my heart racing.

"You're not a burden. Sharing your feelings can be really important, especially when you're dealing with so much," she said softly.

I hesitated, but something about her sincerity made me feel safe. I began to open up about my depression, my thoughts of suicide, and the weight of expectations I carried on my shoulders. "I just feel so alone sometimes, like no one understands what I'm going through."

"You're not alone. It's brave of you to share this, and I want you to know that it's okay to seek help," Ms. Crook said, her eyes filled with compassion.

I nodded, feeling a glimmer of hope amidst the despair. Maybe there was a way out of this darkness.

The next day brought an unexpected wave of betrayal. I walked into Ms. Crook's office to find my parents sitting there, concern etched on their faces. My heart dropped, and I felt exposed, like a deer caught in headlights. Ms. Crook explained my struggles, and their worry was evident.

"Your son is dealing with some serious emotional challenges," Ms. Crook began, her voice calm but firm. "He's expressed feelings of depression and has mentioned thoughts of self-harm."

"What?" my dad exclaimed, his face turning pale. "I didn't know it was this serious."

"I felt betrayed when I came to talk to someone privately about my problems," I interjected, my voice shaky. "I thought I could trust you."

"I understand why you feel that way," Ms. Crook said gently. "But your safety is my top priority. I had to share this with your parents because they need to know how to help you."

I wanted to scream, to run away from the room, but instead, I sat there in silence, feeling like I had lost the one safe space I had found. My parents' faces were filled with concern, but all I could see was betrayal. Looking back now, I understand the importance of their concern. They wanted to ensure my safety and wellbeing, but in that moment, I felt a deep sense of betrayal.

After that meeting, everything changed. The trust I had built with Ms. Crook shattered into a million pieces. I felt exposed and vulnerable, like a tightrope walker who had just lost their balance. Each session with her felt like a chore, a reminder of the trust I had lost. I found myself avoiding eye contact and keeping my responses short.

"Are you okay?" she would ask, genuine concern etched on her face.

"Yeah," I would reply, my tone flat.

"Are you sure? It seems like you're holding back," she encouraged.

I would clench my fists, feeling the anger simmer beneath the surface. "I just don't think this is working anymore," I finally admitted.

"What do you mean?" she asked, her brows furrowing with concern.

"I want to switch counselors," I said firmly. "I don't feel comfortable talking to you anymore."

"Why not?" she probed, hurt flashing across her features.

"Because you told my parents. I trusted you, and you broke that trust. I can't talk to you about anything now," I replied, my voice steady but filled with pain.

"I'm really sorry you feel that way. I had to share it for your safety," she said gently.

"I get that, but it doesn't change how I feel," I said, the weight of my emotions overwhelming me.

"Let's explore this a bit more," she suggested, her voice softening. "Can you tell me what specifically made you feel that way?"

"I just... I just don't want to talk to you anymore," I said, unable to contain my frustration.

"I respect your decision," she said quietly. "If you feel you need a new counselor, I can help you find someone else. I just want what's best for you."

In the days that followed, I navigated the difficult decision to switch counselors. I felt a mixture of relief and guilt, the thought of abandoning the progress I had made with Ms. Crook heavy on my heart. But I needed a fresh start, a safe space where I could truly open up without the fear of being betrayed again.

After a few days of searching, I found a new counselor, Ms. Harris. She had an approachable demeanor, and the moment I walked into her office, I felt a sense of relief wash over me.

"Welcome! I'm Ms. Harris. What brings you here today?" she asked, her tone light and inviting.

"I... I switched counselors. I just needed someone new," I replied, my voice tinged with uncertainty.

"That's perfectly fine! It's important to find someone you feel comfortable with. So, what would you like to talk about?" she encouraged.

I hesitated, feeling vulnerable again. "I guess I just feel really lost. My home life is difficult, and I'm struggling with feelings of depression," I admitted, my voice shaking.

"I'm glad you're here. It takes a lot of courage to seek help. Can you tell me more about what you're feeling?" she asked, her expression compassionate.

As I spoke, I felt the walls I had built around myself begin to crumble. I opened up about my family struggles, the darkness that consumed me, and the feelings of betrayal I experienced with Ms. Crook. Ms. Harris listened attentively, her demeanor reassuring.

"I'm here to support you," she said gently. "You deserve a space where you feel safe to share your feelings. It's okay to be vulnerable."

With Ms. Harris's support, I began to explore new friendships. I reconnected with Carlos, who had been worried about me. "I'm really glad you switched counselors. You deserve someone who gets you," he said, his eyes filled with sincerity.

"Thanks, Carlos. It's been a journey, but I feel like I'm starting to heal," I replied, a genuine smile spreading across my face.

We started hanging out more, supporting each other in our endeavors. He shared his own struggles with anxiety, and I admired his openness. Our bond deepened as we navigated the complexities of adolescence together.

One afternoon, while we were hanging out at the park, Carlos turned to me with a serious expression. "I've been thinking... if you ever feel overwhelmed, just know you can reach out to me anytime. You don't have to go through this alone," he said, his voice steady.

"Thanks, Carlos. That means a lot," I replied, feeling grateful for his friendship. "I'm learning it's okay to ask for help."

As I spent more time with Carlos and my new friends from the support group, I felt a sense of belonging that had eluded me for so long. We shared our experiences, lifted each other up, and celebrated our small victories.

As summer faded into fall, I felt a sense of renewed purpose. I began volunteering at a local mental health organization, sharing my story with others who faced similar struggles. I wanted to let them know they weren't alone.

One day, while leading a support group, a girl named Lisa shared her story. "I feel so lost," she said, her voice trembling. "It's like I'm stuck in this darkness."

"I understand," I replied, feeling a deep connection with her pain. "But there's hope. I was once in that darkness too, but with support, I found my way out."

"Really? How did you do it?" she asked, her eyes wide with curiosity.

"I found people who understood my struggles, like my friends and my counselor, Ms. Harris. It's okay to lean on others," I shared, hoping to inspire her.

That day, I realized how far I had come. I was no longer just a survivor of my struggles; I was becoming a source of strength for others.

As I approached the end of the school year, I felt a sense of accomplishment. My grades improved, and I was more involved in activities that brought me joy. The shadows of my past still lingered, but I learned to navigate them with grace.

Ms. Harris and I continued our sessions, and she encouraged me to think about my future. "Have you thought about what you want to do after high school?" she asked one day.

"I'm considering becoming a counselor," I replied, feeling a spark of excitement. "I want to help others who are going through similar struggles."

"I think that's a wonderful goal," Ms. Harris said, her smile warm. "You have the potential to make a real difference in the lives of others."

I felt a sense of purpose wash over me. The journey was still ongoing, but I was no longer afraid. I had built a support system that I could rely on, and I was ready to embrace whatever came next.

The road to healing is long and winding, filled with twists and turns. But through it all, I learned the importance of seeking help, building connections, and sharing my story. I discovered that I am not alone, and that there is always hope, even in the darkest of times.

Today, I stand taller, more resilient than ever. I'm proud of the progress I've made, and I'm ready to face the future, one step at a time. With the support of my family, friends, and the guidance of my counselors, I am ready to embrace life and all the possibilities it holds.

Resources:

If you or someone you know is struggling with thoughts of self-harm or suicide, please reach out for help. You are not alone, and there are people who care about you. Here are some resources you can reach out to:

National Suicide Prevention Lifeline: 988 – Call or Text

Crisis Text Line: Text "HELLO" to 741741 to connect with a trained crisis counselor

SAMHSA National Helpline: 1-800-662-HELP (1-800-662-4357)

NAMI (National Alliance on Mental Illness): 1-800-950-NAMI (1-800-950-6264)

The Trevor Project: 1-866-488-7386 or text "START" to 678678 for 24/7 crisis support for LGBTQ+ youth

Your life matters, and there is hope for healing. Please reach out to someone who can help you navigate your struggles.

Before high school, race and identity weren't things that I gave much thought to. In my early years, the world was simply the world. I'm not sure if it was my sheltered upbringing or just sheer obliviousness, but those things didn't factor much into my life. Looking back as an adult, I now see what I was blind to then: the jokes, the teasing, and the seemingly innocent remarks from friends and peers that were rooted in something far more insidious. I had grown up in a town with minimal diversity, nestled in a neighborhood filled with families whose roots dug deep into the same land for generations. It was a predominantly white, country community, and while I'd had what I thought was a decent relationship with the neighborhood kids, I was constantly blindsided by the racist comments and jokes they threw my way.

Growing up Latino, specifically Puerto Rican and Italian, made me stick out like a sore thumb. I was darker than the others, with features they deemed "foreign." I remember once playing kickball with the neighborhood kids when someone called out, "Hey, Porta Potty! Beaner! You're up!" At the time, I forced myself to laugh with them. I didn't really understand where these nicknames were coming from, or maybe I did, but I was determined not to let them see that they'd gotten to me. They'd tell me to go back and pick oranges in the fields, and I'd shrug it off, thinking it was just the way things were. I was a kid who just wanted to fit in, so I went along with it, choosing to let the insults wash over me instead of sink in.

Once high school began, though, I started to feel the weight of these labels that had been slapped on me. I found myself caught between two worlds. Among the white kids, I was always the "Spanish" kid, no matter how often I tried to tell them I was also Italian. They'd focus on my Puerto Rican heritage, on what they saw as my Latino features. Meanwhile, the Latino groups in school didn't exactly welcome me with open arms either. Since I didn't speak Spanish, they saw me as an outsider. I'd ask them to help me learn, but the response was always dismissive: "No es mi trabajo enseñarte"—"It's not my job to teach you." I was taking Spanish classes, trying to learn what I could, but it wasn't enough. I needed someone to practice with, but my dad was always on the road, and I couldn't seem to find anyone willing to help me. It left me feeling isolated, caught between two cultures and not fully accepted by either.

Even among other Latino students, those who weren't Puerto Rican seemed to look down on me. They'd refer to Puerto Rican Spanish as broken or less refined, and that made me feel like even more of an outsider. To them, I was a "wannabe," someone who didn't belong. It felt like no matter what I did, I was always straddling the line, never fully accepted as either white or Latino. I couldn't even get the identity checkbox on applications right. To the Caucasian kids, I was strictly Latino, and to the Latino kids, I was just some guy with mixed heritage who didn't really belong.

Finding an inner peace amidst all that was a challenge. I needed to find a way to resolve this identity crisis. I started seeking out friends who would see me for who I was beyond my ethnicity or family background. These friends, who became my chosen family, were more interested in the kind of person I was than in the labels society tried to attach to me. They appreciated my loyalty, friendliness, and work ethic. They looked past the external differences and focused on who I was on the inside.

However, as I grew older and ventured out into the workforce, this inner conflict resurfaced. Suddenly, my identity was being questioned again, this time in the context of job applications. I found myself constantly torn over what to check off in the "race" section. Should I mark "White" or "Hispanic"? With a last name that was unmistakably Spanish, I knew this wasn't a decision I could make lightly. In those days, job applications didn't include the diversity of options they do now—there wasn't a separate "Ethnicity" section that allowed for a more nuanced representation of who I was.

The first few times I applied for jobs and marked "Hispanic," I didn't receive any call-backs. Weeks passed, and I'd watch as the same positions were reposted, one after another. Frustrated and beginning to feel defeated, I decided to reapply, but this time, I marked myself as "White." I was surprised when, almost immediately, I began receiving responses. Calls for interviews and phone screens came flooding in, seemingly out of nowhere. At first, I tried to convince myself it was just a coincidence, that maybe a candidate had dropped out or someone had missed my application the first time around. But after repeating this pattern a few more times, I realized that it wasn't just luck at play.

This experience opened my eyes to the subtle, and sometimes not-so-subtle, ways bias can seep into everyday life. Each time I checked "White" on an application, I felt a pang of guilt, a sense of betraying my own heritage. But I told myself it was a necessary evil, a survival tactic. I'd grown up surrounded by ignorance and prejudice, but I'd also grown resilient. I knew that if I wanted to move forward, I had to find ways to navigate these obstacles, even if it meant compromising a part of myself in the process.

Back in high school, I would hear the names—"Porta Potty", "Beaner", and worse. I'd hide behind a smile, pretending that it didn't bother me, that the words didn't sting as much as they did. I tried to bury my emotions, convincing myself that as long as I didn't show any signs of hurt, the words wouldn't have power over me. But as I entered the workforce and experienced discrimination on a new level, I realized that those words had always left a mark. They'd chipped away at me, little by little, until I could no longer ignore the wounds they'd left behind.

Navigating a world marked by ignorance meant constantly having to find new ways to cope, new strategies to protect myself from the impact of other people's narrow-mindedness. I'd always been taught that you are the average of the five people you spend the most time with. For me, that meant choosing friends who lifted me up, who saw past the labels and embraced me for who I was. They reminded me that there was more to life than fitting into someone else's mold. They taught me to find strength in my identity, to stand tall despite the challenges I faced.

Moving to a new city eventually gave me the fresh start I needed. I left behind the prejudices of my hometown, the limiting beliefs others had imposed on me. I found a diverse community where I didn't have to check a box to fit in, where I could finally explore the full spectrum of my identity without fear of judgment. I embraced my Puerto Rican and Italian roots, celebrating the unique blend of cultures that made me who I am. And in doing so, I discovered a sense of belonging that I'd been searching for my entire life.

Reflecting on those early years, I realize now how much I internalized other people's ignorance. I let their narrow views shape my own perception of who I was, and it took me a long time to unlearn those lessons. But I also see how those experiences shaped me, made me stronger, and gave me a resilience that I carry with me to this day. They taught me the importance of surrounding myself with people who see beyond the surface, who understand that identity is more than just a box to be checked.

So, for anyone who finds themselves caught between worlds, unsure of where they fit in, I offer this: seek out the people who see you for who you truly are, not for what they assume you to be. Surround yourself with those who lift you up and remind you that you are more than the labels society tries to impose on you. Because in the end, it's not about fitting into someone else's definition of who you should be; it's about defining yourself, on your own terms, and finding a community that embraces you for exactly that.

Divorced

At eighteen, during my senior year of high school, everything felt like it was moving at a breakneck pace, and yet, somehow, I'd missed the signs. I'd been so consumed with work, volunteering, and planning for my future that I hadn't even noticed how fractured things had become at home. I barely had time to process that my parents were getting divorced.

It wasn't like the idea of my parents splitting up was new. They'd been struggling for a while, but I guess I'd convinced myself that they'd figure it out. My dad was a hard worker, constantly on the road, doing whatever it took to keep us afloat financially. And, maybe because of that, he wasn't home enough for me to see the strain his absence put on our family. But it all hit me in a tidal wave, and I was completely unprepared for it.

At the time, I had a full plate: school, extracurricular activities, and working as a Certified Nursing Assistant (CNA). Add to that my volunteering with YDC, and I was spread thin, using every opportunity to stay out of the house. I told myself I was just trying to stay busy, to build up my résumé and keep my grades up, but deep down, I knew I was also trying to avoid the negativity brewing at home. I'd always known there was tension, but I chose to ignore the details, almost as if by doing so, I could make them disappear.

The truth was, my parents' relationship had been rocky for as long as I could remember. Arguments were a regular part of life, and I'd learned to tune them out over the years. But things had taken a darker turn recently. My mom was constantly suspicious of my dad's long trips, convinced he was up to something illegal. Whenever the bank statements arrived, she would meticulously comb through them, often finding transactions from random places in other states. It was an endless cycle of accusations and heated confrontations. Once, I even saw my dad grabbing her by the neck, pressing her up against the garage door. It only lasted a moment before he saw me and backed off, but the image was seared into my mind. That was the kind of darkness I was escaping from, and it only pushed me further into my commitments outside of the house.

My mom worked sporadically, usually part-time or temporary gigs that barely required her to leave the house. Her full-time job, as she saw it, was managing the household, but it seemed like more and more, she felt neglected and lonely. She had her suspicions about Dad, and he was too tired to argue or reassure her. On some level, I understood her loneliness, but I couldn't condone how she chose to cope with it. There were rumors that started floating around—whispers in the neighborhood—that my mom was spending a lot of time at our neighbor's house, just a few doors down. I didn't want to believe it, but it seemed like everyone else knew. Eventually, Dad found out, and that was when everything truly began to unravel.

The blow-up was inevitable, but that didn't make it any easier to witness. They fought bitterly, and this time, there was no going back. My mom packed her things, along with my little sister's, and left. She moved in with the neighbor, the very same one everyone had been gossiping about. I was torn. My mom expected me to go with her, to pick up my life and move into some stranger's house. I loved my mom and my sister, but the thought of leaving my dad alone, and my own routines, was too much. I decided to stay with him, though it crushed me to make that choice.

I threw myself even deeper into my work and my activities. There was so much going on that I could almost pretend the split wasn't affecting me. I had midterms coming up, tournaments to train for, CNA hours to fulfill, and college applications to finish. I was busy enough to numb myself to everything, and for a while, it worked. But as graduation approached, the reality began to sink in. This was supposed to be a time of celebration, a rite of passage, but instead, I was caught in the middle of a painful family fracture.

Graduation brought its own set of complications. With only a handful of tickets, I agonized over whom to invite. Could my parents even be in the same room without tearing into each other? I was allotted five tickets, so I chose my mom, my dad, my little sister, and two of my YDC mentors. But my dad insisted that I invite my grandparents, his parents, who I barely spoke to. I didn't want them there. To me, it seemed unnecessary, almost like inviting strangers to something so personal. But Dad wasn't having it. He argued that they'd attended every grandkid's graduation, and this wouldn't be any different.

We fought about it, and in the end, he went over my head and invited them anyway. I felt betrayed, like my own wishes didn't matter. I'd wanted this one thing to go my way, but instead, I was forced to compromise again, sacrificing my own desires for the sake of family obligations. I spoke to my YDC mentors, who, understanding the situation, graciously stepped aside so my grandparents could come. But it left a bitter taste in my mouth, like I had no control over my own life.

Meanwhile, the custody battle over my little sister had begun in full force, dragging me further into the quagmire. Both my parents tried to pull me to their side, wanting me to testify for them in court. I felt suffocated, like they were tearing me apart in their bid to win. But I finally stood my ground, refusing to take sides in a legal battle I wanted no part of. I told them they needed to figure it out themselves. It wasn't fair to put that burden on me.

Even though I managed to stay out of the courtroom, I was still caught in the crossfire. I became the messenger, the go-between for my parents and my sisters. My older sister had long since moved out, and my little sister, now in the middle of a tug-of-war, was too young to understand the complexities. So, the responsibility fell on me to relay messages, coordinate visits, and keep the fragile peace as best I could.

As much as I craved stability, I knew I was clinging to a mirage. I was just as lost as they were, and my distractions were starting to feel like chains. I poured myself into my CNA work, sometimes logging extra hours just to avoid going home. My time at YDC became more than just a commitment; it was my sanctuary, a place where I wasn't defined by my family drama or the choices I had to make. And yet, beneath the surface, I was cracking. The weight of it all—the divorce, the arguments, the constant push and pull—was becoming too much to bear.

Looking back now, I see how badly I needed help. But at the time, I was too wrapped up in the idea that I had to be strong, that I had to handle it on my own. I avoided my dad whenever I could, using his own absences to carve out a semblance of freedom for myself. In those moments, I could breathe, even if just for a little while. It felt like I was always moving, always running, but never getting anywhere.

For a brief period, I enjoyed the sense of freedom that came from the separation. With Dad away for work most of the time, I could finally relax without feeling constantly monitored. I'd use those hours to do what I wanted—watching TV late into the night, inviting friends over, or just sitting in silence. But it was a hollow kind of freedom, and I knew it couldn't last. My life was tethered to the unresolved conflicts at home, and no matter how hard I tried, I couldn't shake them off.

The depression I'd kept at bay for so long began to seep into my daily life. I wasn't sleeping well, barely eating, and I felt an ever-present weight pressing down on me. I still smiled for my friends, put on a brave face at work, and kept up with my volunteering duties, but inside, I was crumbling. Every interaction felt like an act, a mask I wore to keep people from seeing the truth.

In the end, I realized I had to confront the reality I'd been avoiding. My parents' divorce was a turning point, a moment that forced me to face the fact that I couldn't keep running. I was torn between two worlds, and no amount of school or work could change that. I had to find a way to reconcile my past with the future I wanted, even if it meant stepping back from the distractions and facing the pain head-on.

Sloth

I remember the night I decided to dip my toes back into the dating world. The house was quiet—too quiet, really. Since the divorce, I'd gotten used to the quiet. No more yelling, no more tension. Just me. I figured I'd use the free time to explore a little. I'd always been so caught up with work, school, and everything else that dating just...slipped by me. I'd dated Carlos freshman year, but since then? Nothing.

I was a senior now, last semester of high school. I had more free time, kinda. Between my CNA program, work, and volunteering at YDC, I stayed pretty busy. But a little part of me kept itching, like I should try to date again. Problem was, I didn't have a smartphone. I wasn't gonna walk up to some guy at school, especially not in our small town. So, I turned to the internet.

There was this dating site I found, specifically for men. I created a profile—nothing flashy. Just a basic picture of me and a bio that wouldn't make me seem like I was on the menu for everyone to feast on. I didn't need all that attention. Weeks went by, and of course, I got messages. Some were polite, others...well, you'd be surprised how many grown men can be downright nasty. Unsolicited pics, gross comments—nah, I wasn't about that life. I filtered through all that mess until I came across him.

His name was Steven. A little older than me, maybe by a year or two. He was a college student at the nearby tech institute, majoring in biomed. His profile was simple, clean—just like mine. The photo? A bit dorky, but cute. Big brown eyes and full lips, kind of skinny, but he had this awkward charm about him. I don't know what it was, but I was intrigued.

We exchanged some messages. Nothing too deep, just the usual "Hey, how are you?" stuff. Turns out, we had a lot in common. He was focused on school, worked part-time like me, and wasn't just looking for a hookup. We eventually exchanged numbers, and that's how I found myself standing in the pet aisle at Walmart one late evening, waiting to meet Steven in person.

"Is that you?" I heard a voice from behind. I turned around, and there he was—Steven, just like in his photo.

"Yeah, that's me. You must be Steven," I replied, trying to keep my cool.

We awkwardly laughed, and he extended his hand. "Nice to finally meet you."

I shook his hand, feeling a bit more at ease. "Same here. So, what now? Walk around Walmart and pretend it's a date?"

He chuckled. "Well, it's the only place open at this time, so why not?"

We strolled through the aisles, making jokes about the random stuff we'd see. It was strange how comfortable it felt, just walking around and talking about everything and nothing. After about an hour, I asked, "You wanna come back to my place? We can keep talking there, maybe watch something?"

Steven hesitated for a moment before nodding. "Yeah, sure. Why not?"

We headed back to my house, and from there, it felt like time just disappeared. We sat on the couch, laughing, talking about everything from our favorite movies to the weirdest things we've seen on campus. I learned that Steven was originally from Boston, which explained the slight accent he had. He talked about how much he missed the cold winters but didn't mind Florida's warmth either.

"Ever been to Boston?" he asked.

I shook my head. "Nah, I've never left Florida. What's it like?"

"It's beautiful, man. Especially in the fall. Leaves turning colors, that crisp air—it's something else. Maybe one day, you can visit," Steven said, smiling a little.

Before we knew it, the sun was coming up. Six in the morning, and neither of us wanted the night to end. That's when I knew. I really liked Steven, and he seemed to feel the same way.

We started seeing each other regularly after that night. Sometimes, we'd meet at a park, other times we'd just hang out at my place. He introduced me to his friends from college, and I did the same with mine from school and YDC. Our dates weren't fancy—zoo trips, exploring random areas of town—but they were fun. I liked how easy it was with him, how natural it felt.

Summer rolled around, and Steven had to go back home to Massachusetts for a few weeks. It sucked, but we stayed in touch. We talked about everything, and then he hit me with the idea that I should come visit him. At first, I was hesitant. I mean, meet his family? Stay in his childhood home? It felt too soon. But he was persistent, and eventually, I agreed.

The trip was nice, though a bit awkward. His family was friendly, but I didn't expect to spend entire days alone while they all went to work. I figured I'd help around the house, tidy up a bit, but Steven's mom wasn't thrilled about that. Lesson learned—don't mess with someone else's space unless they ask.

On one of the last days of my trip, Steven took the day off, and we went to this gorgeous aquarium and then a lighthouse by the ocean. It was one of those perfect days, the kind that makes you think things are really gonna work out.

But when we got back to Florida, things started to change. Steven moved into an off-campus house with two roommates, and that's when he started pulling away. At first, I thought it was just the stress of school. We were both full-time students, and I had started working more shifts, trying to save up. But Steven—he wasn't the same.

One night, after he'd been acting weird for weeks, we had a talk.

"I feel like I'm not a priority to you anymore," he said, his voice soft but direct.

"What do you mean? I'm just...trying to balance everything," I replied, frustrated but trying to keep calm. "You know I'm working for a reason, right? For us, for the future."

"I get that, but...I don't know. It's hard."

We agreed to try and make more time for each other, but deep down, I knew something was off. He started lying about where he was going, and mutual friends began to whisper that Steven was telling other guys he was single. I didn't want to believe it. I trusted him—or at least I wanted to.

Then, one night, I did something I'm not proud of. Steven was in the shower, and his phone was on the table. I couldn't help it. I went through his texts. And there it was—a conversation with some guy named Alex. They'd been meeting up, sneaking around. My heart sank.

When Steven came back into the room, I tried to give him one last chance.

"Would you ever hurt me?" I asked.

He shook his head. "No, of course not."

"Would you ever cheat on me?"

Again, he said no. But I knew the truth.

"Who's Alex?" I asked, my voice calm but shaking on the inside.

Steven's face dropped. He didn't say a word at first, just stood there, frozen.

"I gave you the chance to be honest," I said, my voice breaking. "And you still lied to me."

All he could do was apologize, but it was too late. I ended it right then and there, and I walked out. The pain was unbearable, but I knew I couldn't stay.

I didn't really know what to do with myself after that night. After I walked out of Steven's place, I drove around town for hours, windows down, letting the summer night air wash over me. But no matter how hard I tried to distract myself, the reality kept crashing down—he'd lied, and worse, he'd cheated. My first real relationship as an adult, and it had all fallen apart.

The next morning, my phone buzzed. Steven.

"Can we talk? Please?" he texted.

I stared at the screen for a minute, then locked the phone and tossed it aside. Talking wasn't going to fix this. Not after everything. But I couldn't escape it either, the questions swirling in my mind. Why did he do it? Wasn't I enough? I couldn't understand it.

That day felt like a blur. I went to work, threw myself into anything that would keep me distracted. But even as I worked, I couldn't shake the hurt. I couldn't escape the feeling of betrayal gnawing at me. My friends told me to keep busy, stay focused on school, but that only worked for so long.

A few days later, Steven showed up at my house. It was late again—he always seemed to show up when the sun was down, like he couldn't face things in the light.

I opened the door, already knowing what this was about. He looked disheveled, like he hadn't slept in days. His eyes were red and puffy, and he barely made eye contact with me.

"Hey," he said, voice barely above a whisper. "Can we...can we talk? Just for a second."

I leaned against the doorframe, crossing my arms. "About what? You've already said everything you needed to with Alex."

Steven winced, running a hand through his messy hair. "I messed up, okay? I know that. But please, just hear me out."

I sighed, stepping back and letting him inside. Part of me was hoping for closure, while another part of me just wanted him to leave.

He sat on the couch, nervously picking at his fingernails. I stayed standing, leaning against the wall. "What do you want to say, Steven? You cheated. There's nothing left to talk about."

"I didn't mean for it to happen like this," he started, his voice shaky. "I didn't even know how to tell you that I...I felt like I was losing you."

"Losing me?" I repeated, incredulous. "You cheated, Steven. You didn't lose me. You just didn't bother to tell me what was going on. Instead, you went behind my back."

"I know! I know..." He rubbed his face in frustration. "It's just... I don't know how to explain it. I was scared. Scared you didn't have time for me anymore. You were always working, always busy. I felt like I didn't matter."

I stared at him, disbelief written all over my face. "So, your solution was to sneak around with some guy and lie to me? That's how you handle feeling insecure? By making me feel like I wasn't enough?"

Steven stayed silent, head hanging low. He looked like he had the weight of the world on his shoulders, but I wasn't going to carry that burden for him.

"I'm sorry," he finally said, his voice cracking. "I'm so sorry, but I...I didn't know how to handle it. I know I hurt you. I hate myself for it."

I didn't know what to say to that. Part of me wanted to yell, to scream at him, to make him feel as awful as I did. But I couldn't. I was tired. So, so tired.

"I just don't get it," I said, my voice softer now, the anger slowly draining away. "Why didn't you just talk to me? You think I wasn't trying? I've been busting my ass, Steven, for us. For a future. I wasn't ignoring you."

"I know, I know. I just... I don't know, man. I was selfish. I wasn't thinking about the future like you were. I just wanted more attention, and instead of talking about it, I went behind your back." His voice was heavy with regret.

There was a long pause between us. Neither of us knew what to say, because we both knew it was over. No amount of apologies or explanations could fix what he had done. My trust was shattered, and that's not something you can just patch up with a few words.

"I don't think there's anything left to say," I finally whispered, looking away. "You made your choice, and I have to live with it. But I can't be with you, Steven. Not after this."

Steven's eyes filled with tears, but he didn't fight me. He didn't argue. He just nodded, accepting the inevitable.

"I'm really sorry," he said one last time, voice cracking. "I hope one day you can forgive me."

"Maybe," I said, turning towards the door. "But not today."

I opened the door, and without looking back, Steven walked out of my life.

For weeks after that, it was like living in a fog. I'd wake up early, head out on my bike before the sun rose, just riding through the empty streets, letting the cool morning air clear my head. My friends tried to help, but they didn't know what to say anymore. They'd told me Steven was trouble, but I didn't listen. I trusted him, trusted that we had something real.

Eventually, the pain started to dull. Steven and I exchanged a few texts over the next few months, mostly small talk, but nothing more. Time had created a gap between us that couldn't be bridged. And maybe that was for the best.

Looking back now, I see it for what it was. A lesson, one of the first real, hard lessons of adulthood. Relationships aren't just about attraction and shared interests. They're about communication, honesty, and mutual respect. And Steven and I, we didn't have that—not the way we needed to.

I don't blame myself anymore for what happened. I was doing what I had to do, working hard to build a future. And I won't lie—I've learned to be more careful with who I trust. But I also know that I deserve someone who respects me enough to be honest, even when things get tough.

In the end, I stood up for myself. I chose not to stay in a situation where I wasn't valued. And that's something I'll carry with me.

Living in a small town, let alone county, it was a surprise to have a popular LGBTQ+ bar like the Cold Keg. Known as the Cold Keg, home of the no keg, it was a staple 7 our little corner of the world. The neon sign outside buzzed faintly, casting a cool blue glow over the cracked pavement.

I remember the first time I went when I turned 18. I was figuring it all out, but that night felt like a whole new world. The loud club music thumped in my chest, drinks clinked, and shots were being downed at the bar. The air was thick with cigarette smoke since, back then, you could still smoke inside. And of course, the drag queens were larger than life—sashaying around like they owned the place.

I started going there every so often. I didn't have much else to do in town, and the Cold Keg was the hotspot, open to everyone, but a true comfort zone for the LGBTQ+ community. No one judged you there. It was where I started feeling like I belonged.

Fast forward to when I was 20. College, bills piling up, and I needed more money—desperately. One weekend afternoon, after tossing around the idea for weeks, I decided to see if the Cold Keg was hiring. I wasn't expecting much, just curious. Maybe I could find something, anything, that would help pay for rent.

I walked through the door, passing the empty ID check area where they would normally card you at night. At the bar, two older guys were deep in conversation. They looked like they belonged—rough around the edges but with an air of ownership. I hesitated for a second, but then I worked up the courage.

"Hey, excuse me. I'm looking for a part-time job," I said, interrupting their chat.

The two men looked up. One was Joe, the assistant manager and DJ, and the other, I recognized as Jojo—the Italian owner of the club. Jojo gave me a long look, his eyes scanning me from head to toe.

"We're not looking for another bartender," Jojo said flatly, lighting a cigarette. His voice had a raspy, old-school New York kind of vibe.

"I'm not picky," I replied quickly. "I'm in college and trying to make ends meet. I'll do anything, really. Whatever I can get."

Jojo squinted at me, taking a drag from his cigarette. "Take off your shirt."

I froze. "Uh, what?"

"Your shirt. Off. Go on." He gestured with his hand, impatient.

It clicked. Some of the guys at the Cold Keg worked the floor in boxers, selling shots. I'd seen them before. They were usually built, toned, and always in the thick of the crowd. I wasn't some bodybuilder, but thanks to high school swimming, tennis, and a bit of dance, I had a lean, fit physique. This could be my shot—no pun intended.

I pulled off my shirt, feeling a bit self-conscious. Jojo and Joe exchanged a glance, nodding slightly.

"You interested in a shot boy position?" Jojo asked, exhaling a cloud of smoke.

"What exactly would I be doing?" I asked, trying to keep my voice steady.

"It's simple. Walk around in boxers, sell shots to the customers. You get a dollar per shot, and the club gets the other. Minimum wage plus tips," Jojo explained, flicking the ash off his cigarette.

Joe chimed in. "You comfortable with that?"

Comfortable? Not exactly. But I needed the money. And this was an opportunity. "Yeah," I nodded. "I can do that."

Jojo grinned. "Good. Be here Friday night. We'll get you started."

Friday came fast. I spent half the week debating what to wear and finally settled on a pair of skimpy boxer shorts I'd bought at a local store. They were tight but not too revealing—just enough to stand out. When I arrived at the club, I was met by the bouncer, a big biker-looking dude with a shaved head and a face like he'd just sucked on a dozen lemons.

"I'm the new shot boy," I said.

He grunted and walked off to confirm with Joe. A minute later, I was allowed inside. I weaved through the packed dance floor, the pulsing lights flashing in time with the beat. Joe was waiting for me in the back office.

"You ready?" he asked, handing me a tray of shots. "Remember, the more you sell, the more you make."

I nodded, my nerves kicking in. I changed into my boxers, feeling the cool air hit my skin, and Joe introduced me to the rest of the staff. The bartenders, dancers, and barbacks all gave me polite nods, though they were clearly focused on their own hustle. I didn't blame them. I was the new guy, and they had their own grind to worry about.

As the night went on, I worked the crowd. At first, it was nerve-wracking—walking around half-naked, trying to get people to buy shots. But after a while, I found a rhythm. The more I sold, the more tips I made. And with every drink sold, the closer I got to paying off some bills.

Still, there were moments that made me question if this was all worth it. Some men were...too friendly. I'd get groped, my personal space invaded, and there were always a few pervs offering me money for private shows. I learned to dodge those, keeping my distance. But it wasn't easy. The longer I worked there, the more I saw how gross people could be.

But there were highlights too—like the themed shows. Three of the performers, Tanya, Anna, and Kelly—known as "Organized Chaos"—

were incredible. Their performances were larger-than-life, the kind of thing that made you forget all the nonsense happening around you.

One night, after a busy shift, the staff gathered at Joe's apartment for a little get-together. Everyone was in good spirits, talking about work and the latest gossip. Jojo surprised me by pulling out a gold chain from his pocket, a Virgin Mary pendant dangling from it.

"You'd look good in gold," he said, handing it to me.

I didn't know what to say. The chain reminded me of my mom wearing a similar one. I smiled and accepted the gift, feeling a lump in my throat. "Thank you," I said quietly, my voice thick with emotion.

In the corner, I noticed Tanya, Kelly, Anna, and Joe huddled together, discussing their next performance. Joe, big mouth that he was, let it slip that I had a bit of dance experience.

"Wait, really?" Tanya turned to me, eyes bright with interest. "You wanna help us with choreography?"

"I mean...sure," I said, suddenly feeling shy. "I'll try my best."

They played a snippet of the song they were struggling with, and before I knew it, I was moving to the beat. It felt natural—just small, isometric movements, but enough to get their attention. When I stopped, the three of them looked at me, wide-eyed.

"Where'd you learn to do that?" Kelly asked, grinning.

"I don't know," I shrugged, still unsure of myself. "Just...felt the music, I guess."

Tanya clapped her hands together, excitement bubbling up. "You're helping us with this one. No question."

And just like that, I became part of the Cold Keg's creative team. I'd help with choreography, sometimes even join in on the performances when they needed extra hands. It was exhausting but exhilarating. And in those moments, up on stage with the lights flashing and the crowd cheering, I felt alive.

This was my new adventure—working at the Cold Keg, balancing school, dance, and the chaos of life. And somehow, in the midst of it all, I was finding myself.

Life at the Cold Keg became a strange blend of excitement, exhaustion, and self-discovery. Friday nights turned into a regular gig—working the floor as a shot boy, watching the dance floor light up under the rainbow of flashing lights, and occasionally dodging the overly touchy customers. But the money was good, and for someone trying to scrape by with rent, groceries, and tuition, it was hard to complain too much.

The real fun, though, was the growing connection I had with the performers—Tanya, Kelly, and Anna. I didn't realize how much I needed that camaraderie until it happened. In a way, they became like family to me, filling the void that had been growing ever since my real family had become more distant. When I moved out on my own, things at home went cold. My mom, bless her, tried to stay in touch, but after a while, the calls came less often.

Tanya, especially, took me under her wing. She was fierce, with a sharp tongue and a heart of gold. We clicked in a way I didn't expect. Maybe it was the shared love of dance, or maybe it was because she saw through the front I put up and knew I was still figuring myself out.

One slow Thursday evening after the bar closed, I stayed behind to help clean up. Tanya was at the bar, sipping on a gin and tonic, still in half her skimpy outfit—makeup flawless, but hair still tied up. She watched me stack chairs and let out a little laugh.

"You know," she started, swirling her drink, "you've got a lot more potential than just slinging shots in your skivvies."

I glanced over, half-smiling. "Yeah? What else would you suggest I do? This is paying the bills."

Tanya shrugged, setting her glass down. "I'm not saying quit. But you've got talent. That little routine you helped us with the other night? You've got the feel for it."

I felt a flush rise to my cheeks. "That was nothing. I was just messing around."

"No," she said, standing up and walking over to me. "You weren't. Trust me, I've been doing this long enough to know when someone's got the rhythm in their bones. You, honey, have got it. Don't let that go to waste."

We talked for a while after that, her leaning against the bar, me with a broom in hand, sweeping up glitter and confetti from the night's show. Tanya wasn't just talking about dance, though. She saw something in me that I hadn't fully acknowledged yet. I was still trying to figure out who I was, what I wanted, and where I fit in the world. The Cold Keg, with all its chaos and craziness, was helping me discover that.

Months passed, and my life at the Cold Keg shifted in ways I couldn't have imagined. What started as a shot boy gig turned into something much more. The shows and choreography became my passion. I was out there, dancing alongside Tanya, Kelly, and Anna, and sometimes even with other friends who would join us for the big performances.

One of the most memorable nights had to be Halloween—our "Heaven versus Hell" show. We were split into angels and demons, and the crowd went wild. The energy was electric. Tanya led us as the dark, brooding queen of the underworld, while Kelly, dressed in white wings and a halo, embodied the sassiest angel you'd ever seen. I was in the middle, balancing between the two worlds, dancing my heart out. It was surreal, knowing I was a part of something this big.

And then there was the glow party—the infamous freak show. I'll never forget the night I got to play a mime. Covered in white paint, a black beret, and suspenders, I silently interacted with the crowd, playing up the character while dancing along to the beat. The next time, I got to step into a more colorful role—Willy Wonka. It was wild, dressed in a bright purple coat, top hat, and glasses, handing out the golden ticket while keeping in rhythm with the group.

Those nights, with the costumes, the makeup, the carefully crafted song mixes, and the elaborate dances, were the golden moments of my time at the Cold Keg. I felt invincible, like I'd found my place. In between the shows, I kept up my usual gig as a shot boy, but now, with my growing popularity, people recognized me from the stage. That recognition translated to more tips—I was walking away with nearly $200 some nights. It was thrilling, but that's when things took a turn.

Joe and Jojo noticed how well I was doing. One night, after the bar had closed and the lights were dimmed, Jojo pulled me aside.

"Listen, kid," he said, lighting a cigarette like he always did. "We're gonna be making some changes. You've been doing great, but from now on, shot boys are going to be tip-based only."

I blinked. "Wait, so… no hourly? Just tips?"

Jojo nodded, his face unreadable in the smoky haze. "It's a business, you know. We gotta make changes where we can."

I tried to keep my cool, but the disappointment hit hard. It felt like a punch to the gut. My enthusiasm for the job began to wane. Without the steady hourly wage, selling shots wasn't as fun anymore. I kept trying, but my heart wasn't in it. Instead of $200, I was lucky to make $20 some nights.

Finally, after much thought, I put in my two weeks' notice. Walking away was bittersweet. I loved the people, the shows, and the memories we'd made, but I needed the money. And with my CNA job picking up over the summer and school weighing on me, it felt like the right move.

Life went on. I focused on school, trying to wrap up my courses at the community college. Working as a CNA was draining, but it kept me busy and paid the bills. Every so often, though, I'd think back to the Cold Keg and wonder what was going on. One day, on a whim, I decided to check in on Jojo. Despite the bitterness I'd felt when they cut my tips, I knew it wasn't personal. It was just business.

I called him up, and after a bit of small talk, Jojo asked me something unexpected.

"You ever think about coming back?" he said, his voice casual. "I could use a bartender, and you're old enough now."

I hesitated. "I've never bartended before, Jojo. I wouldn't know what I'm doing."

He chuckled, his raspy voice full of mischief. "It's not rocket science, kid. We'll teach you. Besides, you'll get the hang of it in no time. What do you say?"

After a few more moments of convincing, I agreed. Part of me missed the place, missed the people. And now that I was of legal age, bartending seemed like a new challenge—something different from my shot boy days. Plus, Jojo had always believed in me, even when I didn't believe in myself.

The following week, I stepped through the doors of the Cold Keg again. The bouncer recognized me and gave me a nod as I walked in. Some things had changed—the team was a mix of old and new faces—but the energy was the same. Tanya, of course, was there, along with Kelly and Anna, and they greeted me like I'd never left.

"You're back!" Tanya exclaimed, pulling me into a hug. "And bartending? Look at you, moving up in the world!"

I grinned. "Yeah, something like that. Just during the slow shifts, though. I'm still learning."

Tanya laughed. "You'll be fine. If you can dance in your underwear for strangers, you can pour a few drinks."

She wasn't wrong. Over the next few weeks, I got the hang of things. Tanya helped me when she could, teaching me the basics—how to mix the popular drinks, handle the cash, and keep the bar running smoothly during the quieter shifts. It wasn't as glamorous as dancing on stage, but it felt good to be part of the team again.

In between bartending, I got back into the shows. They didn't hesitate to invite me back, and it felt like slipping into an old, familiar rhythm. We had our arguments, of course. Spending so much time together, especially under the stress of late nights and demanding customers, tensions ran high. But at the end of the day, we were family. A weird, wonderful, dysfunctional family.

One night, after closing up, we all sat around the bar—me, Tanya, Joe, Kelly, and Anna. Tanya poured us each a drink, even though I could see how tired she was. We talked about life, about the bar, about the future. I looked around at the mismatched group of people I'd come to care about, and I realized something.

For all the ups and downs, for all the craziness and chaos, I'd found my place. Different walks of life, different backgrounds, but at the Cold Keg, we were just people—being ourselves, no pretense, no stress. And that, more than anything, was worth sticking around for.

Resilience

Time flew by in a blur of work, volunteering, and classes. Before I knew it, I was graduating from community college with my associate's degree. University was out of reach financially, so I decided to stick around for another degree, this time in athletic training. I had considered nursing, but after working as a CNA, I saw how overworked and burnt-out most nurses were. My passion for sports and medical care seemed like the best combination for me, and athletic training sounded ideal. Until, of course, I realized that physics and trigonometry were prerequisites, and I just couldn't make sense of why those classes were essential. So, I switched to sports medicine, a similar track that would let me bypass those roadblocks.

With my plans set, I decided it was time to move closer to the university. I spent hours on apartment tours and found a dorm just barely within budget—nothing luxurious, but it was mine, and I was happy to take it. But with my current lease coming to an end, I still had a few months before I could move in. After talking it over with my dad, we agreed I could stay with him for the summer.

One hot afternoon, he came by to help me move. As I packed up the last of my dishes, I heard my dad's heavy footsteps echo down the hallway. He'd been lugging boxes down three flights, muttering about the lack of elevators. When he stepped into the kitchen, he wiped his brow, sighed, and leaned against the counter.

"Taking a break, huh?" I teased, tossing a dish towel in his direction.

"Hey," he smirked, catching the towel. "Not as young as I used to be." He let out a deep breath and looked around the half-emptied kitchen. "So, graduation's right around the corner. Proud of you, you know that?"

I nodded, smiling. "Thanks, Dad. It's been… a long road."

He looked at me, and something flickered in his eyes, like he was trying to muster the courage to ask something. After a pause, he finally spoke.

"Listen, I've been meaning to ask… Why don't you talk to your family much anymore? Your brother and sister—they miss you."

I took a breath and looked away, busying myself by stacking the last of the plates. That question. The one I'd been dodging for years. My stomach twisted, and the walls I'd carefully built felt like they were closing in.

But this time, I didn't want to dodge. I was tired of running. And maybe, just maybe, I was ready to answer.

Setting down the plates, I looked up at him, trying to keep my voice steady. "Dad, I… stopped talking to family because of what you did when I was 15."

He looked taken aback, eyebrows knitting together. "What did I do?"

My heart pounded as I searched for the right words. "I asked you—no, I begged you—not to tell anyone about… about me. About who I am. I wasn't ready. But you went ahead and told everyone anyway." My voice was shaking, but I kept going, the years of hurt rising to the surface. "I didn't feel safe with them knowing. I didn't feel safe with you."

He looked down, his face pale, almost confused. "But… they were happy for you."

"Dad, that's not the point," I whispered, tears starting to well up. "You broke my trust. I came to you with something so personal, so vulnerable, and you just… you made it everyone's business." I wiped my eyes, feeling a familiar ache. "You didn't listen to me."

His face softened, and his eyes began to glisten. For a man who always wore a stoic expression, seeing his eyes water felt like looking at a stranger.

"I'm so sorry, mijo," he said quietly, reaching out to me. "I didn't understand… I didn't think…" He looked down at his hands, helplessly clenching and unclenching. "I never wanted to hurt you."

I bit my lip, unable to hold back anymore. I let him pull me in, and as he hugged me, all the hurt, frustration, and years of walls came crashing down. I sobbed, my shoulders heaving against him as he held me tighter, like he was trying to make up for all the times he hadn't been there.

As we finally pulled back, I laughed through my tears, trying to lighten the moment. "Look at us, getting all emotional."

He chuckled, wiping his eyes. "Yeah, what are we, softies now?" He shook his head, grinning. "Machismo out the window, huh?"

I laughed. "Guess we're rewriting the rulebook."

He looked at me, a soft smile on his face. "Maybe it's time we both left some things in the past, right?"

I nodded, feeling lighter than I had in years. "Yeah, Dad. I think it's time."

And in that moment, I realized I wasn't just packing up my apartment. I was packing up years of pain and hurt, and finally leaving them behind, right where they belonged—in the past.

I'd fully moved back in with my dad, and while it was nice to be somewhere familiar, it also felt strange. My old room was stripped back to basics—a small twin bed wedged up against the wall, a few shelves, and the same worn carpet that I could probably still trace every scuff and scratch on. It was meant to be temporary, just a rest stop while I wrapped up loose ends before heading to my off-campus dorm near the university.

The university itself was just over an hour's drive away, nestled in the middle of the state, a completely different world from the neighborhoods I'd grown up in. I'd spent the last few weeks trying to mentally and physically prepare myself for the change, but then came dance practice the night before orientation, and it threw everything into high gear.

Our dance team was gearing up for a competition, and practices were intense—each movement sharpened, each routine refined until muscle memory took over. Most of the dancers had been together for a while, laughing and chatting as they packed up, but for me, these were still new relationships. I felt a little on the outside, lingering in the shadows as people filtered out. It was just after 2 a.m. by the time we finished, and the drive back home was looking more daunting with every minute that ticked by.

I'd planned for this, though. I grabbed the duffel bag I'd pre-packed with the essentials, walked to my car in the empty parking lot, and leaned the seat back as far as it would go. Streetlights cast a dim, flickering glow over the lot, and I wrapped my jacket into a makeshift pillow. I could hear the distant hum of late-night traffic, muffled yet steady, almost comforting. I closed my eyes and let exhaustion take over, drifting into a light, uneasy sleep with the next day already crowding my mind.

The faint light of dawn woke me. I sat up, groggy but determined, and drove to a nearby grocery store. The fluorescent lights inside were blinding, a sharp contrast to the dim, predawn glow outside. I found the bathroom, splashed cold water on my face, and changed clothes, doing my best to smooth out the creases. I looked at my reflection, catching a glimpse of that tired, determined person staring back at me. It hit me that I was probably going to look and feel like this a lot over the coming months.

I shook off the feeling, reminded myself that I was here to start something new, and headed to campus.

The university's campus was overwhelming, a sprawling maze of brick buildings, green lawns, and towering trees. I kept glancing around, taking it all in, half in awe and half in panic as I tried to make sense of the campus map. Students streamed toward the auditorium for orientation, all chattering with that nervous excitement that comes with the unknown.

Inside, my eyes scanned the rows of seats until I saw a familiar face—an old friend from my youth development days with YDC. My heart lifted instantly. We exchanged grins and grabbed seats together, launching into a rapid-fire catch-up while waiting for orientation to start. In that moment, the crowded, intimidating room didn't feel so overwhelming.

After orientation, we split off to register for classes. My past two years of hard work meant that I was starting as a junior, saving me both time and tuition money. Even so, the price tag of university classes hit hard—way more than community college. I could only afford one class that fit my work schedule and my budget, but it was a start.

One day after class, I was walking around near campus when I spotted a small, nondescript hotel within walking distance from my soon-to-be dorm. It looked quiet, nothing special, but something pulled me inside. It was a long shot, but I was hoping for a job that could help cover my expenses. Inside, I filled out an application, hoping maybe for a position in housekeeping, but they surprised me with an offer to interview for a housekeeping supervisor role. I left that day with a little more hope, and just a few days later, they called to offer me the job. It wasn't the best of pay, but it was a start.

And so, the next six weeks became a test of endurance. Six days a week, I was on the road, driving over an hour each way between my dad's place and the job, managing my work schedule, my one class, and the constant state of exhaustion that threatened to wear me down. Each morning blurred into the next. Some days, I questioned if I'd taken on too much, but I reminded myself that this was temporary—a step on the way to my new life.

The day finally came to move into my off-campus dorm, and my dad came with me to help load everything into the car. As we drove, I looked over at him, thinking about how much he'd been there for me, even when he didn't always understand everything about me or my choices. He stayed silent for most of the drive, occasionally looking over with a proud, almost wistful smile.

Once we arrived, he helped me haul boxes up the narrow stairway, offering advice on how to arrange the room or hang shelves. It was comforting, a small nod to the routines we'd shared in my childhood.

Once everything was unloaded, we stood awkwardly in the doorway. He reached out and pulled me into a hug, holding on longer than usual. "You've got this, mijo. Just remember to call, alright?" His voice was thick with emotion.

"Yeah, of course, Dad," I managed, a half-smile tugging at my lips. We both chuckled, letting the tension ease, and with one last wave, he was gone.

With the room finally mine, I took in the small space: a desk, a bed, and a narrow closet, all freshly organized. It was far from luxurious, but it was mine. I stretched out on the bed, staring up at the blank ceiling, and let myself sink into the quiet.

Here I was, in a new city, with a new job, a new school, and a clean slate. As I lay there, a mix of excitement and nerves churned inside me. I thought about the hard work that got me here, the dreams that lay ahead, and for the first time in a while, I felt a sense of peace, like I was exactly where I was meant to be.

Abandoned

Moving to a new city was a total game changer for me. This place was alive, buzzing past eight p.m., with a kaleidoscope of options for practically everything—food, entertainment, events. It was almost overwhelming but in a good way, as if I'd landed in a place where possibilities stayed wide open, even as the night wore on. Every night offered a different flavor of life here, and it felt like the perfect backdrop for me to do some exploring of my own.

The campus itself was an adventure. I'd spend hours just walking around, taking in the sheer diversity of people. Students of every background, fashion, and interest dotted the pathways, sitting in clusters on the lawns or chatting over coffee, some buried in books, others laughing together between classes. It was like the campus had a pulse of its own, and the more I wandered through its nooks and corners, the more energized I felt. In between classes and work, I'd wander over to places I hadn't seen before—the library tower, the art studios, even some student lounges hidden away in quiet buildings. Each time, it felt like I was uncovering a small piece of this new world, and by extension, discovering something new about myself too.

As the fall semester got rolling, I began to settle into a rhythm, finding a balance between work, school, and what little of a social life I could manage. But to make it all work, I had to hustle, sacrificing my weekends to make sure I could meet my bills. I'd qualified for student loans, but since my family wasn't well off, those loans were my only financial lifeline. Everything else—car insurance, rent, groceries, even small luxuries like having a smartphone—was solely on me.

One night, as I was poring over a mountain of notes and textbooks, I realized that between studying and work, I had barely made any friends. Back in my old town, I'd been the social butterfly, the one who could make anyone smile with just a few words. Here, though, people seemed more guarded. I'd start conversations, sometimes with just a simple "Hey, how's it going?" but more often than not, people would glance at me as though I was invading their personal space. And when it came to talking with women, it felt even more awkward. Most would respond as though I were hitting on them, even though that was the furthest thing from my mind.

After enough failed attempts, I figured out a little trick I came to call "playing the gay card." I don't exactly fit into the stereotypical gay guy image, but I figured it was worth a shot. It was a conscious decision to make it very clear that I wasn't trying to date anyone, just genuinely wanting to connect. And, like clockwork, it worked almost every time.

One early morning, I slid into my seat for an anatomy class and noticed a girl next to me. She had a quirky sense of style—chunky boots, a cropped jacket, and a stack of bracelets jangling on her wrist. She looked so different from everyone else in the room, like someone who lived life on her own terms. Something about her energy intrigued me, and I felt an instant pull to connect.

"Good morning!" I greeted, trying my best to keep it casual. "How's it going?"

She turned slowly, almost too slowly, giving me an icy stare as her eyes took me in from head to toe. I tried not to squirm under her gaze, but she didn't make it easy.

"Hi," she replied flatly before turning back to stare at the front of the empty classroom.

I could have let it go, chalked it up to a failed attempt, and moved on. But something in me wouldn't let this one slide. I took a deep breath, feeling that all-too-familiar nervous excitement, and decided to try again.

This time, I leaned over and turned on what I now call my "gay charm"— not over-the-top, but enough to make a point. "Girl!" I said, lowering my voice conspiratorially. "Let me tell you about this pole dancing class I took the other day—it was so fun. You've got to try it."

Instantly, her demeanor shifted. She whipped her head around, eyes wide with interest. "Oh my God, tell me more!" she said, a smile breaking through her once-stern expression.

I grinned, feeling a spark of excitement. From that moment on, I knew I'd made a friend. Her name was Jocelyn, and as luck would have it, she was also a sports medicine major. We exchanged numbers, and after class, we hung around talking about everything from classes to dance, her adventurous spirit coming through in every sentence.

A few months later, after we'd spent plenty of study sessions and Starbucks runs together, she admitted, "You know, when you first talked to me, I thought you were hitting on me."

I laughed, nodding. "Trust me, you weren't the only one who thought that. Guess I need to work on my non-threatening intro."

"No way," she replied, rolling her eyes. "Thank goodness you brought up that pole dancing class; I'd have never known you were actually just trying to be a friend."

Our friendship was exactly the break I needed, a grounding force in the chaos of college and work. Jocelyn had a knack for knowing just how to make even the longest, dullest study nights feel fun. We'd sit in the back of coffee shops, taking breaks from our work to people-watch, making up wild backstories for everyone who walked by. She even joined me a couple of times on my weekend shifts at the hotel just to keep me company, bringing along notes and snacks as we talked through classes, dissected the latest gossip, and vented about life.

And in the midst of juggling everything—school, work, and friendships— I learned just how tough but rewarding independence could be. While I'd learned to thrive on my own, moments with people like Jocelyn were reminders that I didn't have to go through it all by myself. The weekend shifts, long study hours, and never-ending search for balance started to feel less overwhelming.

One evening, while we sat in my dorm after a particularly rough shift, she looked around at my sparse room with a small frown. "You know," she said, tossing her jacket on my bed and taking a seat, "it's not fair that you're doing this all alone."

"I mean, it's not ideal, but it's part of the whole college experience, right?" I shrugged, grabbing us each a drink from my mini-fridge.

She leaned back, crossing her arms. "But still. No financial help from your parents? I can't imagine doing this without a safety net. Not even, like, once in a while?"

I shook my head. "Nope. My family's... complicated. And money is tight. Besides, it's kind of freeing to know that I'm the one making it work. That I'm getting through this on my own."

Jocelyn's eyes softened as she looked at me. "Well, you've got me now," she said with a playful grin, tapping her drink against mine in a makeshift toast.

"And I'm pretty sure that's worth more than anything else," I replied, grinning back.

The fall semester ended on a high note, with finals passed, and the relief of a break setting in. Jocelyn and I made plans for the holidays, a strange feeling of warmth filling my chest as I realized I was finally beginning to make this city my home.

In those few months, I'd gone from sleeping in my car after dance practice to building a network of friends, a work routine, and an academic life that felt uniquely mine. I'd learned to navigate challenges, lean into my independence, and trust the path that was unfolding before me. And as winter crept in, I felt a growing excitement for what the new year might bring, knowing that whatever happened, I'd meet it head-on, surrounded by friends who'd become family.

Though I was meeting new people, something was missing. I had made a few friends, like Jocelyn, who I met in class after testing the waters with my "gay card," and Chelsea, who was a regular target of my playful teasing on campus. Despite this small circle, I realized I lacked a true connection with any male friends, let alone a gay male friend with whom I could bond in a deeper, more personal way. There was my old boss, Louie, who lived nearby, but he was older and always busy, and my best friend back home, Tere'—or Honeybee, as I affectionately called her—wasn't around. So, as I'd done back in the day, I turned to the apps, hoping to connect with someone new.

Navigating these apps, though, was like stepping into a world that had only grown wilder and more superficial since I last ventured in. I braced myself for the flood of unsolicited photos and the endless barrage of inappropriate requests. After wading through the chaos, I stumbled upon a profile that was refreshingly simple: just a close-up of a friendly face in a baseball hat. His name was CJ, and he had a warm, approachable energy that put me at ease. He didn't jump into anything vulgar or expect anything beyond casual conversation.

After two weeks of chatting, we decided to meet at a local coffee shop. When I arrived, I spotted him sitting outside, waving as he caught sight of me. We ordered drinks, and the conversation flowed effortlessly. We laughed, shared stories, and even joked about the fact that I didn't speak Spanish—something that often made me feel like an outsider. But CJ, instead of judging, offered to teach me. His openness made me feel seen and accepted in a way I hadn't experienced before, especially on such a sensitive topic.

"So, where'd you grow up again?" CJ asked, leaning in as he sipped his latte.

"Small town, middle of nowhere, basically," I chuckled. "I mean, you'd probably think it's cute for like an hour, but then you'd get tired of the early closures and the single diner that everyone goes to."

He laughed. "Sounds... quaint? Maybe not my scene, though. I like a bit more flash."

"Oh, I've noticed!" I teased, glancing at his shiny designer watch and the perfectly coordinated outfit. CJ had a taste for the finer things—a bougier style I admired but never really embraced myself.

Our differences never got in the way, though. We were inseparable, filling our weeks with endless adventures. We both juggled work, classes, and trying to make ends meet, but CJ always brought a level of excitement to our outings. Eventually, we started hitting up the local gay bars together, exploring a nightlife I'd only seen from the other side of the bar when I worked back home. The city's clubs were in a league of their own, packed with energy, featuring dance floors that pulsed with music and outdoor lounges that gave us a breather from the bass-heavy beats inside.

One of our favorite memories was a talent show one Wednesday night. Two drag queens, fierce and fabulous, faced off. The first queen came out dressed as a lion and gave a dramatic performance to a trap remix from The Lion King. She had backup dancers, lighting effects, and a routine that had everyone roaring with laughter and awe. The second queen, a local favorite, performed a trendy pop number and was confident her popularity would secure the win. But CJ and I? We were rooting for our lion queen all the way. When the popular queen took the crown, CJ threw his hands up in disbelief.

"Are you kidding me?" he exclaimed, laughing. "I mean, did they even see the performance she just put on? Lion queen for life!"

For the next five months, Tuesday through Sunday, CJ and I were regulars at every club in town. The music, the people, the routines, and the vibe were always amazing, but after a while, the clubs felt repetitive—same songs, same performers, even the same drinks. So, in a burst of spontaneity, we started taking road trips down south, seeking out new scenes, and with each trip, our friendship grew stronger. His family even welcomed me with open arms, calling me "hermana," just as he did. We were practically family, sharing in each other's lives, crashing at each other's places, and finding endless ways to switch up our routines.

But then, something shifted. The more we hung out, the more territorial CJ seemed to become. He'd interrupt my conversations with other guys at the club or pull me away if I ran into a friend. At first, I thought it was playful jealousy, but after a while, I began to notice how often I was catering to his comfort, overlooking my own connections to make sure he felt included.

One night, Chelsea pulled me aside at a café. "Hey, can I ask you something?" she said, stirring her coffee slowly, her gaze steady on me.

"Shoot," I replied, knowing her well enough to sense that she'd been holding something in.

"Do you think CJ… has feelings for you?"

I almost choked on my drink. "What? No way, he's just… well, he's CJ. Just dramatic, I guess."

Chelsea raised an eyebrow. "I don't know. I've seen him give the death stare to practically every guy who talks to you."

I laughed it off, but her words stuck with me. I didn't believe CJ was interested in me that way. I figured his possessiveness was just part of his personality. But when I met someone new—a guy who genuinely made me happy—CJ's behavior took a strange turn. I shared my dating stories with him, excited to finally talk about someone who brought out the best in me. But instead of cheering me on, CJ grew quieter and more distant.

"Hey, you wanna hit the usual spot tonight?" I texted him one Saturday. No reply. Days turned into weeks, and still nothing. CJ wasn't responding to my calls or messages, and his absence felt like a betrayal. This was my best friend, practically my family. I wondered if he'd just moved on or found someone else. But then I'd see him pop up on dating apps, and a pang of hurt would hit me. He was still around, just… not with me.

I confided in Chelsea one night after class, my frustration spilling out. "I just don't get it. How do you go from being that close to someone to… nothing?"

She offered a sympathetic smile. "People can be complicated, especially when they're dealing with feelings they might not want to admit."

Her words lingered with me. Maybe CJ had felt something I didn't see, or maybe it was my new relationship that made him feel left out. Either way, I'd lost a friend I thought would always be there. I missed the laughter, the late-night trips, and the crazy adventures we shared. But with the chaos of school, work, and my budding relationship, I tried to move forward. Life went on, as it always does, and I threw myself into my routine, determined to focus on the good things ahead.

Losing CJ felt like the rug had been pulled from under me. He had become such an important part of my life, almost like a brother. It was as if we were family, and now, without warning, he was just… gone. Each time I thought about him—each road trip memory, each late-night club adventure, each laugh shared over coffee—there was a sharp pain in my chest, a reminder of what had been. The worst part was that I'd never understand why he disappeared, what triggered his silence, or why he left me behind without a word. I'd been left feeling abandoned in a way that cut deep, like the familiar pain of family walking away during my parents' divorce.

I went through a range of emotions—hurt, confusion, and anger. I tried to distract myself, to bury the pain in work and school, hoping the ache would fade. But the truth was, I had to face the feelings. I knew I'd have to confront that sense of abandonment head-on. To let go of the hurt, I first had to let myself feel it fully.

One night, when I couldn't sleep, I sat down and wrote out everything. I wrote to CJ, expressing the betrayal, the sadness, and the loss. Writing gave me a chance to say all the things I'd never get to say to him in person. As I finished, I felt a weight lift slightly, as if putting those feelings down on paper took away some of their power over me.

I reminded myself that not every friendship, no matter how deep, is meant to last forever. People enter our lives for reasons we don't always understand at the time. CJ had taught me that it's possible to form bonds with people who feel like family, even if those bonds don't last. And while our friendship was over, the memories we'd created would always stay with me.

To finally let go of the pain, I had to forgive CJ in my own heart. I didn't need an apology or an explanation from him; I just needed to make peace with what was. And by releasing that pain, I allowed myself to open up again—to trust, to form new friendships, and to find joy in the present. Letting go was hard, but it was also a reminder that I could keep moving forward, stronger and more open than before.

Complicated

Roberto's message came through on a slow Tuesday evening. The notification buzzed on my phone, interrupting the steady rhythm of some random late-night playlist I'd put on as background noise. Dating apps had always been a mixed bag for me; messages were usually loaded with empty flattery or, worse, a string of requests that made it feel more like a transaction than a conversation. This time, however, his message was surprisingly... normal. Genuine, even. I took a second before opening it, cautious yet curious about whether this would be different.

"Hey! I hope I'm not bothering you, but I just wanted to say you seem really interesting—and, uh, quite good-looking too. I'd love to get to know you better if you're up for it!"

Simple. Direct. Polite. And, honestly, kind of refreshing. I quickly skimmed through his profile again, even though I'd already checked it when I matched with him earlier. His picture was charming; he had this endearing combination of a wide smile, dorky glasses, and a mop of curly hair under a baseball cap. Hispanic, and from his profile, a year younger than me. He had the vibe of someone who was smart, maybe a bit studious, but who knew how to have a good time.

I debated responding. Part of me hesitated, knowing all too well that the reality of these encounters often didn't live up to the initial excitement. But something about his smile in that picture—the way it looked so open and unaffected—made me curious. I tapped on my screen and started typing.

"Hey, Roberto! Not a bother at all. Thanks for the message—made me smile," I typed back, adding a casual smiley face at the end to keep things light.

After hitting send, I waited, a little unsure of what would come next. But the response was quick, as if he'd been waiting. And soon enough, we were trading messages back and forth, bouncing from one topic to another with an ease that was rare for a first conversation. Roberto told me he was in school for his master's degree, working part-time in accounting, and hoping to meet someone he could genuinely connect with. He didn't say it directly, but there was something in his words that hinted he'd been through his own share of disappointing encounters, too.

"Feels like it's hard to meet people who aren't just looking for something superficial," he'd typed, an ellipsis hanging at the end, as if he were half-expecting me to disagree.

I nodded at my screen, as though he could see me. "Tell me about it! It's hard finding anyone who just wants to be real these days," I replied.

After a few minutes, he sent another message. "Are you into coffee?"

I chuckled at the casual shift. "Isn't everyone?"

"Good point. Well… if you'd be up for it, maybe we could meet up for a coffee sometime? Just as friends—no pressure!"

It took me a moment to process that. There was something disarming about his approach, and that, somehow, made it feel like he was actually interested in knowing me beyond a brief chat. I bit my lip, feeling a small flutter of nervousness that I hadn't felt in a while, and responded with a simple, "Sure. Coffee sounds great."

We set a date for Wednesday evening. The whole thing was low-pressure, yet I could feel a mixture of excitement and nerves building up as the day drew closer. The day of our meeting, I found myself rehearsing things to say, half-worried I'd come across as awkward or that the connection we'd felt through the screen wouldn't translate in person.

The coffee shop we'd chosen was one of those cozy, slightly rustic places with exposed brick walls and plenty of tables squeezed close together. The smell of fresh espresso hung in the air as I entered, and it immediately put me at ease. Roberto was already there, waiting by the counter, looking exactly like his picture—except, to my surprise, he was a little taller than I'd imagined. He had on the same dorky glasses from his profile photo, which only added to his charm.

He smiled when he saw me. "Hey! Glad you made it," he said, his voice warm and unassuming.

I felt my nerves ease instantly. "Wouldn't miss it," I replied, grinning back.

We ordered our drinks—an iced latte for me, black coffee for him—and found a table in the corner, where it was quiet enough to talk but still surrounded by the comforting buzz of the cafe. As soon as we settled in, conversation came naturally, flowing with the ease that only happens with certain people. We started with the usual topics—school, work, hobbies—but it didn't feel like small talk. It felt... genuine. He listened attentively when I talked, nodding along and asking thoughtful questions that made me feel seen in a way I hadn't in a long time.

"So, tell me," Roberto said, leaning forward with a playful glint in his eye, "What's one thing about you that wouldn't be obvious just from looking?"

I laughed, caught off guard by the question. "Wow, diving right in, aren't we?" I teased, taking a sip of my drink. "Alright... well, I have a bit of an anime obsession. Don't judge," I added quickly, half-expecting him to laugh.

Instead, he grinned wide. "You're kidding! I'm probably one of the biggest anime fans you'll ever meet. I've literally re-watched Attack on Titan three times."

My jaw dropped. "You're serious? I mean, that's commitment! Okay, so what's your favorite anime, then?"

We spent the next hour geeking out over our favorite shows, laughing and arguing over which series had the best storylines or character arcs. From anime, we somehow segued into fitness, then into life goals, then into childhood memories. Time flew by in a way it rarely did, and before I knew it, we'd emptied our cups and the cafe was starting to thin out.

Roberto glanced at his watch, looking a little disappointed. "I hate to end this, but I actually have an early class tomorrow," he said, his smile slightly sheepish.

"Yeah, I get it," I replied, feeling a twinge of reluctance myself. "But hey, this was… really fun."

"It was," he agreed, his gaze softening. He hesitated, then added, "Would it be weird if I asked for a goodbye kiss?"

My heart skipped a beat, and my mind went into overdrive. I'd never kissed anyone on a first date—it always felt like too much, too soon. But something about this moment, about him, made me want to throw that rule out the window. After a second's pause, I nodded.

Roberto leaned in, his hand gently resting on my shoulder as our lips met. The kiss was soft, tender, and brief, yet it felt like a spark igniting between us. We pulled away, sharing a shy smile, and he murmured, "Text me when you get home, okay?"

"Will do," I replied, still a bit dazed.

As I drove back home, I couldn't stop smiling. The whole experience felt surreal, like something out of a story rather than my own life. And as I replayed the night in my mind, I couldn't help but feel a surge of hope. For the first time in a long time, I felt like I'd met someone who genuinely wanted to know me, who was interested in more than just a surface-level connection.

The following days were filled with messages, short phone calls, and more late-night chats. Each time, I found myself learning more about Roberto. He told me about his family, his struggles balancing work and school, and the little quirks that made him who he was. And I shared, too—my past relationships, my ambitions, the things that scared me. It was like peeling back layers of myself, bit by bit, and finding comfort in his understanding.

We started seeing each other regularly, going on casual dates and discovering new places around town. Each moment felt effortless, as if we'd known each other far longer than we actually had. And gradually, without me even realizing it, Roberto had become someone I genuinely cared for—someone I wanted to keep in my life, no matter where things went.

One evening, a couple of weeks in, he invited me over to his place. It wasn't a grand affair; he didn't make it feel like a big step, even though I knew it was. He'd just said, "Hey, come over, we can pick a show to binge and order some food," and somehow, it felt like the most natural thing in the world.

As I walked into his small one-bedroom apartment, slightly cluttered with moving boxes as his ex moved out, I felt a strange mixture of comfort and nervousness. But the evening turned out to be everything I hadn't even known I wanted. We laughed, shared snacks, argued over the best episodes of our show, and just… existed together, without any pressure or pretense.

And as the months passed, that feeling of being truly seen and valued only grew stronger. With Roberto, everything felt like it fell into place effortlessly, as if all the pieces of our lives had been waiting for this moment to finally fit together.

As the weeks turned into months, Roberto and I settled into a rhythm that was as comforting as it was exciting. There was an ease to being with him that I hadn't felt in previous relationships, a sense of security that allowed me to open up in ways I didn't expect. We both had demanding schedules, but somehow, we always found time for each other. Whether it was an evening at his place with takeout and our favorite show or a quick coffee date squeezed between work and classes, every moment felt meaningful.

One night, as we lay on his couch, half-watching our series and half-lost in conversation, Roberto turned to me with that soft smile of his and said, "You know, I don't think I've been this happy in a while." His voice was gentle, almost as if he were afraid to admit it out loud.

The vulnerability in his words struck a chord. "I feel the same," I replied, reaching for his hand. "It's like… I don't have to try so hard to be understood with you."

He nodded, his thumb brushing softly against my knuckles. "Exactly. I mean, it's rare to find someone who just gets it, you know? Who just feels… right."

That moment, with the two of us lying there, hands entwined, I felt a warmth spreading through me. It was a profound, quiet kind of happiness—the kind that doesn't announce itself loudly but settles in your bones and makes everything feel lighter.

By the time the holidays rolled around, I was fully immersed in my busy schedule, balancing multiple jobs to keep up with my finances. Roberto understood the pressures of juggling work and responsibilities and often reminded me to take it easy, which made me feel even closer to him. I'd grown up accustomed to handling things on my own, so having someone who genuinely cared about my well-being felt like a luxury I hadn't experienced before.

One evening, Roberto messaged me with a proposition that set my nerves tingling. "Hey! My friends and I are getting together at my parents' place for a game night. I'd love for you to come if you're up for it."

Meeting someone's friends is a milestone in any relationship, and though I was nervous, I knew I wanted to be part of his world. After all, he had become such a huge part of mine. With a bit of excitement and a dash of trepidation, I messaged him back, agreeing to join. The idea of seeing him in his element, surrounded by his friends, filled me with a sense of anticipation.

The day of the game night, I managed to get off work a bit early, grateful for the understanding boss who allowed me to leave. I drove over to his parents' house with a mixture of excitement and anxiety bubbling within me.

When I arrived, Roberto was already at the door waiting. He greeted me with a quick kiss, his eyes lighting up when he saw me. "You made it," he said, his voice warm and welcoming, easing some of my nerves.

I took a deep breath as he guided me inside. His parents' home was beautifully decorated—warm, inviting, and impeccably clean. The kind of place that felt lived-in but also well cared for. We walked into the living area, where his friends were gathered, laughing and chatting as they prepped snacks and arranged games. Roberto introduced me to each of them, his hand resting reassuringly on my back as he did.

His friends were easygoing and welcoming, and soon enough, I found myself laughing along with them, feeling like I belonged. There was an ease among them, a familiarity that comes from years of friendship, and I felt a pang of envy mixed with admiration. This was what I had always hoped to find in a friend group—a sense of warmth and shared history. Roberto's friends were like his second family, and it was beautiful to witness.

As the night went on, I became more comfortable, joining in on the games and chatting with Roberto's friends about everything from work to our favorite TV shows. At one point, Roberto wrapped an arm around my shoulder, and I leaned into him, feeling utterly content.

When the night wound down, I found myself reflecting on how significant this experience had been. Meeting Roberto's friends had given me a glimpse into a life I hadn't fully imagined for myself—a life where relationships, both romantic and platonic, were filled with laughter, warmth, and a genuine sense of belonging. And with Roberto by my side, I realized that maybe, just maybe, that life was within reach.

As Roberto and I grew closer, life's everyday challenges didn't disappear, but facing them felt more manageable with him by my side. I continued working long hours to make ends meet, sometimes feeling overwhelmed by the demands of balancing my finances and planning for the future. Roberto was there every step of the way, offering support in the small, unassuming ways that meant the world to me.

One evening, after a particularly exhausting day at work, I confided in him about my financial struggles. "It's just… a lot sometimes," I admitted, my voice barely above a whisper. "I want to be stable, to build something meaningful, but it feels like I'm constantly running uphill."

Roberto listened quietly, his eyes filled with empathy. "You don't have to carry it all alone," he said softly. "I'm here for you, and I believe in what you're building. It's okay to lean on someone once in a while."

Hearing those words felt like a weight lifting off my shoulders. I'd always prided myself on being independent, but with Roberto, I felt safe enough to let my guard down. For the first time in a long time, I allowed myself to believe that I didn't have to face life's challenges alone.

Things were going well for us, and I was feeling more secure in our relationship than ever. But life has a way of throwing curveballs when you least expect them. One afternoon, Roberto texted me with some unexpected news: his ex had reached out, asking to come by and pick up the last of his belongings from Roberto's apartment.

Roberto explained it casually, assuring me there was nothing to worry about, but a knot of anxiety formed in my stomach. I trusted Roberto completely, but the idea of his ex re-entering his life, even briefly, brought up insecurities I hadn't realized I still carried.

"I just wanted to let you know," he said during our next phone call, his tone calm and reassuring. "There's nothing between us anymore, but I didn't want you to feel blindsided or worried."

I took a deep breath, grateful for his honesty. "Thank you for telling me. I trust you, Roberto. It's just… I guess I have my own insecurities. I don't want to feel like I'm competing with anyone."

Roberto's voice softened. "You're not competing with anyone, I promise. I'm with you because I want to be, because I care about you."

His reassurance calmed my nerves, and as I listened to his words, I felt a renewed sense of trust. Roberto wasn't the type to keep secrets or play games, and in that moment, I knew our relationship was built on a foundation of honesty and mutual respect.

The holidays came and went, and before we knew it, a new year had begun. Roberto and I celebrated together, toasting to new beginnings and reflecting on everything we'd shared. Looking back, it was incredible to think about how much our lives had intertwined in such a short period. Roberto wasn't just my boyfriend—he was my confidant, my partner, my best friend.

As we settled into the new year, we continued to make memories, from small, quiet evenings at home to spontaneous weekend getaways. Each experience added another layer to our relationship, deepening our bond and making me feel more certain than ever that I'd found someone truly special.

One evening, as we sat on his couch, Roberto took my hand and looked into my eyes. "I'm not usually one for making big declarations, but... I want you to know that I'm committed to building something real with you. You're not just a part of my life—you're becoming the most important part."

His words filled me with a warmth that was indescribable. "I feel the same way," I replied, my voice barely a whisper. "I want us to build something lasting, too."

In that moment, I knew that no matter what challenges lay ahead, we would face them together. Roberto wasn't just someone I was dating; he was someone I wanted to share my life with, someone I wanted to grow alongside.

As our relationship continued to evolve, I found myself reflecting on how much had changed since that first message on a dating app. Roberto had brought light into my life, showing me a love that was genuine, supportive, and filled with joy. He'd shown me the beauty of vulnerability, the strength of shared dreams, and the power of a love built on trust.

Looking ahead, I knew that our journey was just beginning. There would be challenges, moments of doubt, and times when life tested our bond. But with Roberto by my side, I felt ready to face whatever came our way. After all, love is not just a feeling—it's a choice, one that we would continue to make, day after day, as we built our future together.

The start of the new year felt like a fresh chapter in every possible way. Roberto and I had celebrated so many milestones in just a few short weeks: I'd graduated from university, we both landed incredible new jobs, and I'd moved into a beautiful apartment with my friend Jocelyn. Roberto was now just a few buildings over in the same apartment complex. It felt surreal, like everything we'd worked so hard for was finally coming together.

I had left my old job with the school system and had started working for a local nonprofit, a position that meant a lot to me because I was finally in a place where I could make a difference and feel valued. Roberto, meanwhile, left his position at the bank and secured an accounting job downtown. We were both so thrilled for each other's accomplishments, frequently toasting over quiet dinners and dreaming up a future that felt more tangible every day. Things were truly looking up.

One Friday evening, as we settled into the weekend's routines, Roberto told me he'd been invited out for drinks with some of his new coworkers. "They're planning to hit up a few places after work," he said with a grin. I could see the excitement in his eyes; he wanted to fit in and bond with them. I smiled, encouraging him, "You should go! Celebrate with them and have a drink for me," I said. "Just let me know if you need a ride back. I don't want you drinking and driving."

"Of course," he said, kissing my forehead. "I'll text you if it gets too late or if I need a ride. Thanks, babe."

As the night went on, I enjoyed a peaceful evening at home with Jocelyn, catching up on our favorite shows and chatting about everything from work to weekend plans. Our apartment was cozy, and I found myself appreciating the calm, knowing Roberto was just a few buildings away. Everything felt in its place.

Later in the evening, my phone buzzed. It was Roberto calling, and I was surprised by how loud it was wherever he was. After we exchanged a few pleasantries, he mentioned that some of his coworkers wanted to continue the night at one of their places. "They're thinking of going back to Brian's," he said, sounding slightly hesitant. "You know, to hang out and… smoke some weed."

There was a pause on my end. While I trusted Roberto, the idea of him getting high at some stranger's house was unsettling to me. "I don't know, Roberto… I know you're having fun, but this just makes me uncomfortable," I said, hoping he'd take my concerns to heart.

"I'll be fine!" he replied with a slight edge in his voice, brushing it off as if it was nothing. "It's just one night, and everyone's going. We're just unwinding a bit, that's all."

A part of me wanted to insist, to ask him to come home, but I decided to let it go, hoping he'd be responsible and keep my feelings in mind. After all, relationships require trust, and I knew he was just trying to bond with his new coworkers. "Alright, just be safe," I said, forcing myself to sound supportive, though a small knot of unease had settled in my stomach.

It was well past midnight, and I was still up, checking my phone every so often. I couldn't sleep, my mind filled with mixed feelings. Finally, my phone rang again, and it was Roberto. He sounded more than just tipsy—his words were slurred, and he admitted he'd gotten a bit high on top of drinking.

"Hey, babe, I think I'll just crash here," he said. "Brian's place is closer anyway, and I'm in no shape to drive back. I'll see you tomorrow."

My heart sank. I knew Roberto had already made his mind up, and there was a dismissiveness in his tone that I couldn't ignore. "Roberto… I just don't feel good about this. It's late, you're not in your right mind, and I'd feel better if you came home."

But he dismissed me again, his voice relaxed, almost patronizing. "Babe, it's no big deal. I don't know why you're so worried. I told you I'm fine here."

As the call ended, I was left staring at my screen, frustration brewing. Unsure if I was overreacting, I reached out to my friend Louie, hoping for some perspective. "Am I crazy for being upset?" I texted. "Roberto is spending the night at a coworker's place—one he barely knows—because he's high and drunk. It just doesn't sit right with me."

Louie replied almost immediately, reassuring me. "You're not crazy at all. He's crossing a line, especially after you expressed how uncomfortable you felt. He should respect that."

With that validation, I texted Roberto, telling him to send me his location so I could pick him up. After a few messages back and forth, he finally sent his address, reluctantly giving in. I threw on a jacket and drove over, my mind racing. I pulled up to a house that looked quiet, and as I walked up to the front door, I noticed how eerily empty the place felt.

When I knocked, Roberto opened the door with a bleary expression, smelling of alcohol and marijuana. There was no one else in sight except him and his male coworker, who barely acknowledged my presence. My frustration deepened as I took in the scene, but I kept my cool, refusing to argue. "Let's go," I said simply, and Roberto followed me back to the car.

The car ride was silent. He was in no state to talk, and I knew that trying to discuss it now would be pointless. Once we got back to his apartment, I helped him to his room, tucked him in, and left without saying another word. The whole night had left me feeling dismissed, hurt, and deeply disappointed. Roberto had communicated his plans, but where was the consideration for my feelings? I lay awake that night, feeling the sting of his disregard.

The next morning, I knocked on Roberto's door, determined to have a serious conversation. He greeted me with a half-hearted apology, his eyes tired and avoiding mine. "Look, I'm sorry if I worried you, but Brian's place really was just closer, and I didn't think it was that big of a deal."

"Roberto," I said, taking a deep breath. "It's not just about where you stayed. You knew how uncomfortable I felt, and you dismissed me. You didn't take my feelings into account at all."

He sighed, brushing it off. "It's not like I did anything wrong. I didn't cheat or do anything disrespectful. I just had a bit of fun, okay? I don't get why you're making this into such a big thing."

I felt my frustration building, and I had to steady my voice. "It's not about that. It's about respect and boundaries. When you're in a relationship, you can't just act as if you're the only one who matters. It's about considering each other."

He shrugged, clearly not understanding the weight of my words. "Fine. I get it, okay? Next time, I'll just make sure you're more comfortable. Can we drop it?"

But it wasn't that simple. The issue wasn't just this one night; it was his complete dismissal of my feelings. We went back and forth, each of us standing our ground, but every word he said felt like a wall being built between us. Finally, we came to a strained understanding. He promised to be more mindful, and I reluctantly agreed to move past it. But inside, I felt a shift—a quiet resignation I hadn't expected.

After that day, I found myself growing more and more reserved. Where we once laughed and shared our days openly, I now held back, unwilling to risk being dismissed again. Roberto noticed the change, though he didn't address it directly, and the dynamic between us began to feel strained.

He tried to bring up small talk, make plans, or crack jokes, but I couldn't shake the lingering resentment. Every time I thought about how quickly he had brushed off my feelings, it was like a weight in my chest. Roberto had been such a source of joy, but now, I felt myself holding back, putting up barriers I never thought I'd need with him.

I thought about how much had changed since the start of the new year, how the bright and hopeful beginnings now felt clouded by tension. And I wondered if this rift was something we could truly bridge or if it would grow wider, eventually pulling us apart.

In those quiet moments alone, I questioned what I wanted from this relationship. Roberto and I had once dreamed of a future together, but could that future exist if respect and understanding weren't part of the foundation?

Days turned into weeks, and while we tried to move forward, there was an unspoken distance between us. Roberto acted like everything was fine, trying to rekindle the warmth we once shared, but deep down, I couldn't ignore the gnawing feeling that something was fundamentally broken.

And as I reflected on where we were headed, I realized that love alone might not be enough to keep us together if the respect and trust we needed to thrive were no longer there.

Over the next few months, things seemed to be alright with Roberto. We slipped into a rhythm that felt good. We'd made it past a few rocky moments, had our good times to lean on, and I was hopeful that the conflicts we faced were simply growing pains, something temporary that we could iron out with time.

To celebrate his birthday, we got out of town for a weekend with his friends, exploring the city with a carefree, celebratory vibe. Roberto was in his element, laughing, joking, and radiating energy. Being around his friends brought out a warmth in him that I sometimes missed when it was just the two of us. But seeing him like that reassured me. After all, if his friends saw something so great in him, it validated what I was holding onto.

Our summer continued in that same carefree style. We spent weekends checking out new places, finding little hole-in-the-wall cafes, and taking impromptu road trips. Roberto started traveling more for work, visiting clients in other states, and I missed him when he was gone, but he made up for it with texts and calls. The distance added a sense of excitement when he returned, and I found myself swept up in a renewed closeness. It felt like everything was aligning, as if this phase was exactly where we were meant to be. My doubts faded, and I leaned into the trust that we were growing together, adapting to each other's lives and temperaments.

By fall, he invited me along on one of his work trips to Chicago. It sounded perfect—an escape together, and a chance to experience one of his client trips firsthand. During the days, while he worked, I explored the city on my own. I hadn't expected to feel so lonely, but I put it down to being in an unfamiliar place, on his turf. Evenings, though, were the highlight. The anticipation of him finishing work kept me going all day, and our dinner reservations or simple walks by the lake afterward filled those nights with a sense of closeness.

One night, Roberto booked a table at an upscale restaurant. He seemed excited, and I tried to mirror his enthusiasm, though I'd never been anywhere so elegant. White tablecloths, chandeliers, and the murmurs of refined, quiet conversation made me feel self-conscious. As the night went on, my stomach twisted. This was his world, but I felt out of place—like a puzzle piece that didn't quite fit. My thoughts spiraled. Roberto was chatting easily with the waiter, and I couldn't shake the feeling that I was only partially there, an observer in a space that wasn't mine.

"I'll be back in a minute," I murmured, slipping away and heading toward the restroom, fumbling for my phone. I needed to vent, to let it out somehow, so I called a friend, my voice low as I explained the pang of not belonging, the strangeness of it all.

"Maybe it's a bit of an overreaction," my friend said kindly. "But it's just nerves. Let him know—it's about communication."

Returning to the table, I tried to look calm, but Roberto caught my tension. The evening ended with tension in the air and a silence that felt too thick to break. Back at the hotel, it came to a head. Roberto looked at me and asked, "Why did you get so worked up? It was just dinner."

I tried to explain, but my words came out jumbled. Rather than understanding, he seemed irritated, and his impatience only fed my frustration. The night ended in silence.

But by the next day, things seemed better. Roberto softened, apologizing in his own way, and we decided to put it behind us. Halloween came soon after, and we dressed up in matching costumes for a party, laughing as our friends admired the effort we'd put in. Friendsgiving was another highlight, our apartment filled with our closest friends, laughter, and plates of food that left us full for days. By the time December rolled around, we'd taken a trip to San Diego, and everything felt beautifully right.

Then came his work's Christmas party. He'd mentioned the event offhandedly, but I was excited. Another chance to connect with his world, to maybe make him proud by blending in seamlessly this time. The restaurant was stunning, decked out with festive decorations, and the people seemed friendly. As I settled into the evening, I found myself laughing and chatting with the couple beside me, easing into the night with a drink in hand. We got caught up in a conversation that had us roaring with laughter, and I felt more at ease than ever—until Roberto leaned over and whispered in my ear.

"Read the room. You're being extra," he said, his tone light but laced with irritation.

I froze, my laughter cut short, and I set my drink down, my mood plummeting. I scanned the table, noticing the subdued tones of the other conversations. Roberto was right—the couple and I had gotten a little too loud. The old sense of not fitting crept back, and I fell quiet for the rest of the meal, determined to stay present for Roberto's sake.

After dinner, we moved on to a vintage-style bar with a lovely, intimate atmosphere. The music was perfect, and for a while, I forgot my earlier embarrassment. Roberto, however, was drinking steadily, his demeanor loosening as the night wore on. I decided to hold off on more drinks, but I stayed close, laughing with his friends and trying to join in. But as the night deepened, Roberto's friends gathered around him, and I felt more and more like an outsider.

An hour passed, and I leaned over, my voice gentle. "I'm going to head back soon. I'm ready for bed."

Roberto turned to me, visibly tipsy, and his face crumpled in disappointment. "No! I don't want you to leave," he muttered, his tone a mix of frustration and childish insistence.

"I'll be back at the hotel," I said quietly, but his face darkened, and suddenly he was stomping his feet like a child, drawing stares from those around us. Embarrassment washed over me as I tried to keep my voice level.

The crowded elevator ride down was silent except for Roberto's heavy breathing, his chest rising and falling like he was fighting to keep himself composed. When we stepped outside, my Uber canceled, and I knew it'd be a walk to the quieter side of town.

I was hoping the cold air would help him sober up, but instead, his demeanor shifted from sadness to anger. He began shoving his shoulder against mine, his posture aggressive.

"So, you want to go, huh?" he sneered, his voice low and bitter. "Then go! Let's go, right now."

My patience shattered. Something in me broke, and I exploded, my voice coming out sharper than I'd ever heard it before. "I'm leaving, Roberto!" I shouted, the finality of my words hanging in the air.

His face morphed in surprise, and he followed me as I walked briskly, his breaths coming in angry huffs. I needed to expel my anger somehow, and in a rare moment of rage, I punched the wall, feeling the impact reverberate up my arm.

Roberto fell silent, his anger seemingly dampened by my outburst. We walked back to the hotel in silence, our footsteps the only sound between us.

The next morning, Roberto's texts started early. He wanted to talk, but I ignored him, focusing on my work, trying to steady myself. But when I returned to my apartment, he was there, waiting by my door. His face was a mix of regret and exhaustion, and I sighed, unlocking the door and grabbing my dog, Jeter's leash.

"Let's go to the dog park," I suggested, leading the way in silence.

Once we reached the park, Roberto began apologizing, his voice thick with guilt. I listened, letting his words settle before speaking. "I just need a day," I told him quietly, "to cool off, to get some space."

Roberto nodded, his expression tense but understanding. "I get it," he said. "I'm sorry. I didn't mean to ruin things."

I left him at the park, walking home alone and feeling a strange mixture of relief and heaviness. Over the next day, memories of our good times replayed in my mind. They softened my anger, weaving a nostalgic ache into my heart that made me question if maybe I was holding onto only the highlights and ignoring the harsh reality of our fights.

The months passed, and while Roberto and I were still together, things had undeniably changed. Our once-easy rapport was now strained, punctuated by arguments that often felt like repeats of old grievances. I found myself swallowing my words to keep the peace, silencing my frustrations to avoid sparking more fights. The good times, the things I clung to, felt like echoes of a past we were slowly drifting away from. Then, just when I thought I could endure the strain, it happened.

The day I finally dialed Roberto's number to end things was one I never thought would come. The tension had been building in every corner of my mind and body, and I couldn't hold it in any longer. With each ring, I felt my resolve slipping, but the moment he picked up, the words tumbled out before I could reconsider. "Roberto, we need to break up."

I'd planned to end things in person, but the dam of frustration had burst. All the things I'd been bottling up – the endless arguments, his lack of respect for boundaries, the way he would twist every disagreement back onto me – came pouring out. Roberto's voice broke through, pleading for another chance. "Please," he begged, his voice rough and desperate, "let's talk about this when I get back." I could hear the heartbreak in his voice, and for a moment, I almost reconsidered. But I'd reached my breaking point, and I didn't know if I could pretend to be okay anymore.

A few days later, Roberto returned. I felt a glimmer of hope as we sat down to talk, something rare in our recent conversations. We went back and forth, my words carrying a depth of honesty and a request for something more, while Roberto seemed ready to finally listen. "All I'm asking for is to feel like I'm being heard," I said, my voice strained. "I need boundaries, and I need us to take each other's needs seriously."

Roberto nodded, and for the first time, I saw him acknowledge the reality of what I was saying. "I get it. I know I've messed up. I just... I don't know how to fix it. But I want to try." We agreed to take some space, each of us working to improve things from a distance. I wanted to believe we'd found a path forward.

But in the months that followed, our relationship became a relentless roller coaster. Every high was punctuated by a deep low; moments of laughter and closeness were quickly overshadowed by petty arguments and unresolved issues. Yet in November, there was a night that felt different. We sat across from each other at a quiet café, and for the first time in what felt like forever, we talked without any walls up. I told him about my need for healthier boundaries, and he actually listened, nodding thoughtfully as I spoke. For once, he shared his concerns without making me feel small. The weight lifted between us, and for the first time in months, I felt hopeful.

The next month and a half were almost surreal in their calmness. Roberto and I were back to our old selves – laughing, spending lazy evenings together, and genuinely enjoying each other's company. I started to believe that we'd finally turned a corner.

Christmas Eve arrived, and we planned a cozy night in. Roberto came over with groceries, smiling as he set them down on the counter. We joked around, chatting about our plans, and I suggested he come to my sister's for Christmas, given that his family was out of town. He hesitated, looking slightly uncomfortable before saying, "Actually, my friend Jean's in town, and we're planning to hang out at my parents' place."

I felt a pang of disappointment but nodded, understanding. Still, something felt off. His face was tight, his eyes avoiding mine. "Roberto, are you okay?" I asked softly.

He looked at me, his gaze shadowed, and said, "I don't think I want to be in a relationship anymore."

The words hit me like a tidal wave. I swallowed, trying to keep my voice steady, even though my insides were collapsing. "But... we were doing so well. Why now?"

Roberto's eyes were damp, but he didn't seem to have an answer. "I just don't want this anymore." And just like that, he walked out, leaving me standing there in shock. I barely made it to the couch before the tears broke free. The loneliness of that night, and the days that followed, felt like a weight I'd never shake off.

The months passed in a blur of sleepless nights and constant, aching confusion. I couldn't understand how something that had seemed to be healing had fallen apart so fast. By the time February rolled around, I'd mustered enough courage to reach out to Roberto, hoping for a bit of closure.

We exchanged light texts, and I found myself asking him to meet up for coffee. He declined, his response leaving me stunned: "You hurt me too much. That's why I don't want to meet."

I read the text over and over, trying to make sense of it. "How did I hurt you?" I replied, my heart racing.

"Because you broke up with me," he answered.

The conversation ended there, but my thoughts spiraled, replaying every argument and tender moment we'd shared. It made no sense; we'd agreed to work on things, yet he acted as if I'd wronged him irreparably. I couldn't shake the feeling that I was caught in a web of miscommunication, but there was no way to untangle it now.

A few days later, my coworker suggested a quick lunch break to lift my spirits. We laughed and chatted as we entered a nearby fast-food restaurant, but my heart dropped when I spotted Roberto in line. He looked up, catching my eye, and offered a stiff smile. I approached him, managing a casual, "Hey."

Roberto pulled me in for a brief side hug, his greeting cold. I felt the words bubbling up before I could stop them. "I don't understand what you meant the other day, about me hurting you. I thought we were okay?"

He rolled his eyes, exasperation flooding his face. "This again?" he said, his tone sharp. "Can we just not do this?"

His response stung, but I pushed on, desperate for clarity. "I just don't get it. We worked so hard – I thought we'd moved past it all."

Roberto's voice rose, his face reddening. "Leave me alone!" he snapped, his words echoing in the crowded restaurant. Heads turned, and I felt a wave of embarrassment wash over me as Roberto's anger filled the room. My coworker stepped forward, her expression protective, but I put a hand on her arm and turned to leave. My cheeks burned as I walked away, Roberto's last words ringing in my ears.

That was the final time I saw him.

The emotional weight of that day left me feeling raw and humiliated. Roberto had been my confidant, my friend, my partner, but our story had devolved into something unrecognizable. What had once been a bond full of laughter and love had become tangled in miscommunication, resentment, and regret. I spent the following weeks reflecting on everything that had transpired. I replayed conversations, arguments, and tender moments alike, trying to piece together where we'd gone wrong.

As I moved forward, two lessons surfaced, clear and inescapable. The first was to never be afraid to set boundaries. If my partner couldn't honor them, then maybe they weren't the right person for me. The second was to prioritize self-respect. I'd spent so much energy holding onto the past and trying to fit myself into Roberto's world that I'd forgotten my own worth.

Healing didn't come overnight, but each day I felt a little lighter. The heartbreak no longer defined me; I was finally learning to carry my past without letting it weigh me down. I couldn't change what had happened, but I could choose to honor myself moving forward. That was enough – and perhaps, in the end, that was everything.

Therapy

It's easy to look back at moments in life and gloss over the details, focusing instead on the outcomes. But when I think back to the first time therapy became a vital thread in my life, the details are sharp, vivid, and sometimes haunting. It all began during my time at university—a chapter where my independence was fresh, but my emotional stability was fragile.

The holidays were always the hardest. Each year, I found myself caught in the tug-of-war between my mom and dad, who both wanted me at their respective homes. "You're coming to my place first, right?" my mom would say, her voice laced with that subtle guilt-trip tone. "I mean, you always go to your dad's longer than mine."

My dad, on the other hand, was no less strategic. "Don't forget, we're having your favorite dessert this year. And I expect you'll stay late enough to help clean up this time."

No matter how carefully I tried to split my time, one of them would find a way to make me feel like I'd failed. Each visit ended with an undercurrent of resentment, leaving me emotionally drained. It wasn't until one particularly long drive back to their small town that I noticed a pattern: the closer I got, the more the anxiety settled in, like a lead weight pressing on my chest.

Growing up in a town so small it could suffocate you, I always had one goal—escape. Moving to the nearest large city felt like a victory, even if it was just a couple of hours away. That distance represented freedom. But returning, even for a short visit, made me feel like I was being pulled back into a black hole.

I'd done everything in my power to leave that place behind. Most of the people I went to high school with were still there, living lives that suited them but would have suffocated me. There's nothing wrong with staying put if it works for you, but I knew I needed to see what the world had to offer. That drive, though—long, dark, and quiet—had a way of dredging up every fear I thought I'd left behind.

One night, it became too much. I was speeding, doing 80 mph down a stretch of highway with no streetlights and no one else on the road. The thoughts started creeping in, uninvited and relentless.

What if you just didn't go back?

It was a whisper at first, but it grew louder. What if you just turned the wheel? The idea of ending it all seemed, in that moment, like an escape from everything—the expectations, the guilt, the crushing weight of feeling like I'd failed before I'd even really begun. My heart pounded against my ribcage as the thought took root.

This wasn't the first time I'd felt this way. When I was younger, I'd flirted with the darkness, but back then, I didn't fully understand what it meant. Now, I knew exactly what was happening, and it terrified me. I had worked too hard to get here, to build a life beyond that small town. Was I really going to throw it all away?

The thought was interrupted by a spark of clarity. You don't have to do this. You can reach out. You can get help. With shaking hands, I picked up my phone and dialed the suicide hotline. The phone barely rang before a calm, steady voice answered.

"This is the suicide hotline. My name is Claire. How can I help you today?"

The moment I heard her voice, everything broke loose. I started crying, the kind of deep, guttural sobs that had been building for years. I couldn't even get a word out.

"It's okay," Claire said softly. "Take your time. I'm here. Just breathe."

I followed her instructions, taking in shaky breaths until the sobs subsided enough for me to speak. "I... I was going to drive off the road," I admitted, my voice trembling. "I didn't want to go home, and the thought just... it felt easier than facing everything."

"Thank you for telling me that," Claire said, her tone gentle but firm. "You made a brave decision to call before taking any action. Let's talk about what's going on. What's making you feel this way?"

The floodgates opened. I told her everything—the pressure from my parents, the fear of failure, the suffocating anxiety that came with returning to my hometown. Claire listened without interrupting, her occasional "I understand" or "That must feel so heavy" reminding me I wasn't alone.

When I finished, there was a long pause before she spoke again. "It sounds like you've been carrying a lot on your own for a long time. You're doing so much, and it's okay to feel overwhelmed. But it doesn't have to end here. There's help available for you."

Her words were like a lifeline. She told me about resources I could access, including therapists in my area. "Talking to someone regularly can help you untangle some of these feelings," she said. "And if you ever feel this way again, please call us. You don't have to go through this alone."

By the time we hung up, the urge to hurt myself had passed. I sat in my car, tears still streaming down my face, but for the first time in a long time, I felt understood. I'd been heard, and that made all the difference.

The next day, I woke up with a plan. The lingering weight of the night before was still there, but so was a new resolve. Therapy felt like the lifeline I needed, and I was determined to find a way to start. After breakfast, I reached out to my university advisor to see if there were any therapists available on campus. The advisor was supportive, mentioning a student counseling center that provided services to full-time students.

Relief flooded through me—this was exactly the opportunity I needed. I grabbed my skateboard and cruised across campus to the center. The sun was warm against my skin, and I tried to let the rhythmic clack of my wheels on the pavement soothe my nerves. When I arrived, the student staff greeted me with kind smiles, and their friendliness helped ease some of the tension building in my chest.

To my surprise, they had an opening that afternoon. I couldn't believe how quickly things were falling into place. I scheduled the appointment, making a mental note of how much time I had to attend my morning class, grab lunch, and return. As I left the center, a small knot of anxiety curled in my stomach, but I kept reminding myself that this was the right step forward.

Hours later, I found myself back in the quiet lobby of the counseling center. My earlier confidence had waned, replaced by a nervous energy that left me fidgeting in my seat. My mind was racing with doubts. What if I can't open up? What if the therapist judges me? What if I can't make sense of what I'm feeling?

The sound of a door opening interrupted my spiraling thoughts. A warm voice called out, "Pasado!"

There was no going back now. I stood up, legs trembling slightly, and followed the voice into a cozy, dimly lit office. The walls were adorned with colorful, abstract artwork that immediately caught my attention. It felt personal, like someone had poured pieces of themselves into this space.

"Hi, I'm Dr. Patel," the man said with a friendly smile. He gestured toward a plush couch, and I sat down, feeling awkward yet hopeful.

"First sessions are pretty straightforward," Dr. Patel explained, his tone calm and approachable. "We'll talk about what brought you here and discuss what you might want to focus on in therapy. Today's more about getting to know each other; the deeper work usually begins in later sessions."

I nodded, unsure of how to respond but appreciating his honesty. He asked me about my background and what had prompted me to seek therapy. Slowly, haltingly at first, I began to share. I told him about the anxiety that had overwhelmed me on my drive back to my parents' town, the way I felt caught between my mom and dad's constant tug-of-war, and my deep-seated fear of failure and being trapped in a small-town life I never wanted.

As I spoke, I noticed how intently Dr. Patel listened. He didn't interrupt or rush me, and his gentle affirmations—"That must have been really difficult" or "I can see how that would feel overwhelming"—made me feel understood in a way I hadn't expected. By the time the session ended, I was shocked at how quickly the hour had flown by.

"That's a good start," Dr. Patel said as I stood to leave. "You've been through a lot, and I think we can work through some of these feelings together. See you next time?"

I nodded, managing a small smile. "Yeah. See you next time."

Over the semester, I saw Dr. Patel at least once a month. Therapy quickly became a safe space where I could unpack the layers of my life—growing up in an abusive household, the pressure of always being the "middleman" during my parents' divorce, and the relentless fear of falling short. While the sessions were free for full-time students, finding time in my packed schedule was a challenge. Between multiple jobs and a full course load, I often felt like I was running on fumes. But I made it work because I knew how much I needed it.

By the time we reached our fourth session, the weight I carried felt a little lighter. I was starting to open up more, to trust Dr. Patel and the process. Each session was a step forward, and I was eager for our fifth meeting.

The summer semester rolled around, and I decided to take a lighter load—just two classes—to give myself a break. I figured it was a chance to catch my breath after all the work I'd been putting in. Therapy, however, was still a priority.

On the day of my appointment, I walked into the counseling center feeling ready to dive deeper. At the check-in desk, the student worker greeted me with a polite smile and asked, "Are you currently enrolled full-time?"

The question caught me off guard. "No," I replied hesitantly. "I'm only taking two classes this semester."

Her smile faltered slightly. "I'm sorry, but only full-time students have access to therapy services. We can allow you to see the therapist for a quarter of a session today, but after that, you'll need to find resources elsewhere."

I stood there, frozen, as the words sank in. Disappointment and frustration welled up inside me. I had just started to feel comfortable with Dr. Patel, and now I had to start over? It felt unfair, but I knew arguing wouldn't change anything. "Okay," I murmured, trying to keep my voice steady.

When Dr. Patel called me into his office, I could see he already knew about the situation. "I'm sorry about this," he said, his tone sympathetic. "I understand how difficult it is to build a rapport with someone and then have to start fresh. Unfortunately, the policy is out of my hands. But I do have some resources for therapists in the area who can continue working with you."

I appreciated his understanding, but it didn't make the goodbye any easier. "I was just starting to feel like I was making progress," I admitted, my voice tinged with frustration.

"I know," Dr. Patel said gently. "And I'm proud of the work you've done so far. I hope you'll take these resources and keep going. Therapy isn't about any one person—it's about you and your journey."

We said our goodbyes, and I left his office with a mix of gratitude and sadness. Once outside, I pulled out the list of therapists he'd given me and dialed the first number. Starting over wasn't what I wanted, but I wasn't about to give up on the progress I'd made. Therapy had become too important to me, and I knew this was just another step in the journey.

The first resource I called was a behavioral health center. The term itself gave me pause. Behavioral health? Isn't that where they treat... crazy people? The thought was reflexive, and as soon as it crossed my mind, I felt a twinge of guilt. That's not fair, I corrected myself. If Dr. Patel thought this place could help me, there must be a good reason.

I took a deep breath and dialed the number. After navigating a surprisingly straightforward menu, a friendly voice answered on the other end. "Thank you for calling Harmony Behavioral Health. How may I assist you?"

"I... uh, I was referred by my campus therapist," I said, my words a bit shaky. "I wanted to see if I could set up an appointment."

"Of course! Do you have insurance?" the representative asked.

"Yes," I replied, quickly rattling off my provider information. To my relief, she confirmed that they accepted my insurance. After some back-and-forth to find a time that worked, she scheduled me for an appointment the following week with a Dr. Hill.

Once the call ended, I felt a small wave of relief. But also curiosity. Who was Dr. Hill? That evening, I did some research. She had a robust set of credentials and an impressive history of working with patients facing challenges similar to mine. The reviews were glowing, with many praising her compassionate and solution-focused approach. It gave me hope. Why not give it a shot?

The week dragged by, anticipation building with each day. When the appointment finally arrived, I found myself driving to a small town just outside of campus. The address led me to a mostly empty plaza with cracked asphalt and faded storefront signs. It looked... less than inviting. I hesitated for a moment, gripping the steering wheel and questioning whether I was in the right place.

Therapy is about pushing through discomfort, I reminded myself. With that, I parked, took a deep breath, and walked inside.

The lobby was clean but cold, both in temperature and atmosphere. I checked in at the desk and took a seat, pulling my jacket tighter as I waited. After what felt like forever, I heard my name: "Pasado!"

I looked up to see a petite woman with short blonde hair and a casual outfit that seemed to say, I'm approachable. This was Dr. Hill.

"Hi, I'm Dr. Hill," she said with a smile as she gestured for me to follow her. Her office was simple but welcoming, with calming tones and small personal touches like framed quotes and a plant on the desk. Still, I felt my nerves spike. Starting over was tough. I had to open up again, recount everything, and hope it worked this time.

Dr. Hill must have sensed my hesitation because as soon as we sat down, she spoke gently. "First sessions are more about getting to know each other," she explained. "I'll ask some general questions and get a sense of where you'd like to focus. Have you been in therapy before?"

I told her about my sessions with Dr. Patel and why they had to end. She nodded thoughtfully, then said something that struck a chord: "Therapy is a lot like car shopping. Sometimes the first pick works out perfectly, and other times you need a few test drives to find the right fit. It's okay to explore what feels best for you."

Her analogy clicked instantly. It gave me permission to stop seeing this as a failure if it didn't work and focus on the process instead. Still, the question lingered in my mind: Will she be the right therapist for me?

For the next hour, I revisited the stories I'd shared with Dr. Patel: my struggles with family abuse, the pressures of being the middleman in my parents' divorce, my lifestyle, and even darker moments like suicidal thoughts. Dr. Hill listened intently, occasionally jotting notes but always making me feel heard. By the end of the session, she handed me a brief questionnaire.

"This will help us track your progress," she explained. "If you're comfortable with how today went, feel free to schedule another session."

I paused, reflecting on the hour we'd just shared. To my surprise, I felt more at ease with her than I had during my first meeting with Dr. Patel. Dr. Hill was warm, understanding, and encouraging. I decided then and there to continue with her.

Over the next five years, Dr. Hill became a cornerstone of my personal growth. She was everything I needed in a therapist—insightful, patient, and equipped with tools that helped me navigate both my past and present. She gave me the courage to confront my parents and set boundaries. For the first time, I told them to handle their own issues instead of dragging me into the middle of their disputes. To my shock, they didn't retaliate. Instead, they slowly backed off.

Dr. Hill also introduced me to gratitude exercises, something I hadn't realized I needed. I'd always been hard on myself, quick to see my flaws and failures but blind to my strengths. Through her guidance, I began practicing self-compassion. Small moments of gratitude started to reshape my mindset.

She helped me identify unhealthy social dynamics as well. I had a habit of pretending to be someone I wasn't to fit in or gain approval. Dr. Hill challenged me to embrace authenticity, reminding me that true friendships are built on acceptance, not performance.

One of the most impactful lessons she taught me was the value of maintaining a Positive Mental Attitude (PMA). "It's okay to have bad days," she said during one session. "But try to find the silver lining. Even small wins count." Her words became a mantra for me, a way to reframe challenges and focus on progress rather than setbacks.

There were times when life threw new obstacles my way, like transitioning between jobs and losing insurance coverage. I worried about how I'd afford therapy, but Dr. Hill showed incredible compassion. After explaining my financial situation, she offered me a discounted payment plan, ensuring I could continue our sessions without breaking the bank.

When appointments had to be delayed, I turned to outside resources like Psych2Go on YouTube, which offered bite-sized insights into mental health. I also discovered Alux, a channel focused on personal development and self-help. Through them, I was introduced to impactful books and concepts that complemented the work I was doing with Dr. Hill.

Dr. Hill didn't just help me unpack my past; she equipped me to handle the present. When workplace dynamics at my nonprofit job became overwhelming, she offered strategies to navigate conflicts and maintain my peace of mind. Her guidance extended to my personal relationships, showing me how to communicate effectively and set healthy boundaries.

Transitioning to a new therapist had been daunting, but looking back, I was grateful I took the leap. Therapy wasn't always easy, but it gave me the tools to build a stronger, healthier version of myself.

To anyone considering therapy, I can only say this: It's worth it. Therapy is a journey of self-discovery and healing, and the right therapist can make all the difference. Resources like Psych2Go and Alux are great complements, offering insights that deepen your understanding of yourself and the world around you. Don't be afraid to seek help, it's one of the bravest and most rewarding things you can do.

Rediscovered

Bringing it back to 2018, Dr. Hill had become more than just my therapist, she was my guide through the most complex and vulnerable parts of my life. One of her most significant contributions was helping me process the downfall of my relationship with Roberto. It wasn't an easy task. I had loved him deeply, but in our final months together, things became toxic. Through our sessions, Dr. Hill helped me reflect on our actions and behaviors, not just his but mine too.

"What do you think was the turning point for you two?" she asked during one session, her voice calm and nonjudgmental.

I sighed, staring at the soft beige carpet beneath my feet. "I think… I gave too much of myself to him. I tried to mold my life to fit his, but I never felt like it was reciprocated. It felt normal at the time, but now, looking back, I realize how exhausting it was."

Dr. Hill nodded. "That's a common experience in relationships where one person overextends themselves. It's not about blame but understanding patterns. What does a balanced relationship look like for you?"

Her question lingered in my mind for days after. A balanced relationship? I hadn't even thought about that before. For years, I had measured relationships by how much I could give, not by what I deserved in return. Through these reflections, I started to recognize my worth and what I truly desired in a partner. I also began improving my communication skills, learning to express my needs instead of assuming they didn't matter. Listening had always been a strength of mine, but I now understood that communication required balance—both giving and receiving.

Outside of therapy, however, life felt like it was on autopilot. I was juggling multiple jobs, coming home to an empty apartment, and falling into a monotonous routine that left me feeling hollow. My social life had all but disappeared, and the silence at the end of each day was deafening. One evening, as I stared at my phone, I decided to reach out to old friends.

I started with casual texts, sending simple "Hey, how've you been?" messages to people I hadn't spoken to in years. To my surprise, most responded warmly, happy to reconnect. One of them was Chester, a guy I'd met shortly after high school. He had always been ambitious, focused on college, and had eventually moved to New York City.

"Hey, Chester! How's life in the big city?" I typed.

His reply came quickly. "Busy but amazing! How about you? Been forever."

We exchanged a few texts before I casually mentioned I'd been thinking about visiting NYC. To my surprise, he immediately offered me a place to stay. "If you're serious, you're welcome to crash at my apartment. I've got a pullout couch, but it's comfy!"

I hesitated for only a moment before deciding. Why not? This could be the shake-up I desperately needed. Over the next few months, Chester and I stayed in touch, not just catching up but planning my trip. It felt exciting to have something to look forward to, a chance to step out of my routine and explore the world beyond my small bubble.

When the big day arrived, I boarded the plane with equal parts excitement and nerves. Flying into LaGuardia, I felt the first rush of adrenaline. The sprawling city stretched out beneath me, its skyline a mix of glimmering skyscrapers and endless movement. Once I landed, I grabbed a taxi to Chester's apartment, marveling at the chaos of the streets. Yellow cabs honked incessantly, people moved with purpose, and the sheer scale of the city was overwhelming.

Chester greeted me with a warm hug at his apartment door. "Welcome to the city that never sleeps!" he said, laughing as he gestured for me to put down my bags.

The apartment was small but cozy, with an eclectic mix of furniture and a faint smell of freshly brewed coffee. "You hungry?" he asked. "There's this great spot around the corner."

We walked to a nearby diner, and over burgers and fries, Chester filled me in on his life. He'd graduated and was now working at a local hospital. "It's demanding, but I love it," he said. "I've also been traveling a lot—Europe, South America, you name it."

His stories were captivating, and I found myself inspired by the life he'd built. It was a stark contrast to how stagnant I'd been feeling. "That's the kind of lifestyle I want," I admitted.

"You'll get there," he said confidently. "It's all about taking the first step."

Chester warned me that his work schedule would keep him busy during my stay, but he promised to take me out at night. In the meantime, I'd have to explore the city on my own. The thought intimidated me at first, but I reminded myself this trip was about stepping out of my comfort zone.

After dinner, he handed me a spare key. "Here you go. The city's yours to conquer."

The next morning, I set out alone, armed with a subway map and a vague itinerary. New York City was everything I imagined and more. I wandered through Central Park, marveling at its vastness and how it felt like a serene oasis amidst the urban chaos. I visited Nintendo World in Midtown, indulging my inner child and feeling a spark of joy I hadn't felt in ages. But it was Washington Square Park that truly stole my heart. The mix of street performers, artists, and everyday New Yorkers gave the space a vibrancy that resonated with me. It became my favorite spot, a place where I felt alive and connected.

One afternoon, I reached out to a cousin on my mother's side who lived in New Jersey. We hadn't spoken in years, but I figured it was worth a shot. To my surprise, she was thrilled to hear from me, and we spent the day catching up over coffee. It felt good to reconnect, a reminder that even distant family ties could be meaningful.

I also decided to try something new: hopping on apps to meet people. While these platforms were often used for dating, I approached them with the intention of making friends. That's how I met Yogi, a lively and kind-hearted guy who instantly clicked with me. We spent an evening exploring the city together, sharing stories and laughter that felt effortless.

By the time my trip ended, I felt like a different person. Traveling solo had been terrifying at first, but it turned into a journey of self-discovery and empowerment. It showed me how much there was to see, learn, and experience in the world. I returned home with a renewed sense of purpose and a clearer vision of the life I wanted to build.

Over the next few months, I stayed in close contact with my friends, riding the momentum of my trip to New York City. Each conversation felt like a lifeline, a reminder that I didn't have to navigate life alone. While catching up with friends gave me a sense of belonging, there was something deeper I was gearing up for—a trip to Colorado for my younger sister's culinary school graduation.

The excitement of seeing her graduate was mixed with an undercurrent of anxiety. My brother and oldest sister would be there as well. I hadn't seen either of them in person since I was ten years old, and after shutting everyone out at fifteen, I'd done little to repair those bridges. They were part of "everyone" I'd excluded from my life, and I wasn't sure how to face them now.

Colorado couldn't come fast enough. When I landed, the crisp mountain air greeted me, a stark contrast to the sweltering summers I was used to. My dad had taken charge of booking the Airbnb for the trip, his first attempt at using the platform. Let's just say it showed. The place was... "interesting." No air conditioning, a quirky layout, and furnishings that looked like they belonged to someone's eccentric grandmother.

"Didn't the listing mention this place didn't have AC?" I asked my dad as I walked through the creaky front door.

He scratched his head, looking sheepish. "Well, it did say 'mountain breeze cooling,' but I thought that was just fancy talk for AC."

Despite the accommodations, the real tension lay elsewhere. My brother and older sister and I exchanged short hellos when we arrived. They stuck to one side of the room, and I found myself retreating to another. The distance wasn't physical—it was emotional, a chasm built over years of silence and avoidance.

The ceremony itself was beautiful but brief. My sister beamed with pride as she accepted her diploma, her love for the culinary arts evident in the way she carried herself. I couldn't help but feel a surge of pride, mixed with a pang of guilt for not being more present in her journey. After the ceremony, we headed back to her place, where she insisted on cooking for us.

"Time for me to show off my skills," she said, tying her chef's apron with a flourish.

The meal was incredible—roasted duck with a cherry glaze, truffle mashed potatoes, and a salad that tasted like it came from a five-star restaurant. It was the kind of meal that silenced the table, everyone too busy savoring the food to talk. For a moment, the tension lifted, replaced by laughter and compliments as my sister soaked up the praise.

That night, after dinner, I noticed my brother and older sister step outside. They weren't exactly subtle about it, holding small, familiar-looking items in their hands. I realized they were partaking in something Colorado was famous for—its "Recreational activities." It was something I had never tried before, but in that moment, it felt like an opportunity.

I stepped outside, hesitant but determined. "Mind if I join?" I asked, my voice shaky but steady enough.

Both of them looked up, their expressions a mix of surprise and skepticism. My brother laughed. "You? Really?"

"Yeah, really," I said, settling into one of the patio chairs.

The initial conversation was small talk—how the ceremony went, how long they'd been in Colorado, the quirks of the Airbnb. Slowly, the walls began to come down. The topic shifted to memories, to the years we'd missed out on each other's lives.

"You know," my sister began, "we didn't really know how to reach you after everything. It felt like you didn't want us in your life."

"I didn't know how to let anyone in," I admitted, my voice barely above a whisper. "Back then, it was easier to shut everyone out than face everything I was feeling."

My brother nodded, his eyes softening. "We've all made mistakes. But we're here now."

For the first time in years, I felt a genuine connection with them. We talked late into the night, the air thick with unspoken forgiveness and a sense of starting over. That night marked a turning point. The distance that had once defined our relationship didn't feel insurmountable anymore.

The next day, we decided to visit the Garden of the Gods, a breathtaking park known for its towering red rock formations. Walking through the trails, we marveled at the beauty around us. The sunlight danced on the rocks, casting shadows that shifted with the wind.

"This is incredible," I said, snapping a photo of one particularly stunning view.

"It's one of my favorite places," my sister chimed in. "I used to come here to clear my head when school got overwhelming."

The hike felt therapeutic, the perfect backdrop for our budding reconnection. We laughed, joked, and even took a silly family selfie, the kind where everyone's trying not to squint in the sun. It was a day filled with moments that reminded me of what I'd been missing.

As the trip came to an end, I said my goodbyes and headed to the airport. My next destination? New York City for World Pride 2019. Yogi had been hyping it up for months, and I couldn't wait to experience it firsthand. The energy in the city was electric, the streets packed with people from all walks of life celebrating love, diversity, and acceptance.

The parade was a whirlwind of color and sound. I had the honor of opening the parade with my friends, walking hand in hand as the crowd cheered us on. The streets were alive with music, laughter, and an overwhelming sense of community. Everywhere I looked, there were stories of resilience and joy.

We danced, we sang, and we celebrated until our voices were hoarse and our feet ached. One particularly memorable moment was stopping by a drag show in the Village, where the performers brought the house down with their charisma and talent. It was the kind of event that left me buzzing with energy, even as the night wore on.

While in the area, I decided to make the most of my trip. I visited my brother, meeting his wife and my niece and nephew for the first time. The kids were full of energy, peppering me with questions about my life and telling me all about theirs. It felt like a small but significant step toward rebuilding that relationship.

I also reconnected with cousins I hadn't seen in years and even visited my grandfather. Sitting in his cozy apartment, listening to his stories about our family's history, I felt a deep sense of belonging.

On top of that, I met even more genuine friends—people who reminded me of the importance of authenticity and connection. Each interaction was a reminder of how much I'd been missing out on by keeping my world so small.

As the plane took off from LaGuardia, I stared out the window, the city's skyline growing smaller and smaller. Tears welled up in my eyes, and I let them fall. I hadn't expected to feel so deeply attached to the city, but it had become a place of self-discovery and growth for me. The culture, the people, the energy—it all felt like a piece of me I'd been searching for.

Back home, I carried that inspiration with me. I was determined to continue building relationships with my family, meeting new people, and putting myself in a position to someday relocate to New York City. The trip had shown me that life is richer when it's shared, and I was ready to embrace it fully.

Queen

It all started with a shift in mindset. I had been working at my nonprofit job for nearly two years, pouring my heart and soul into a cause I truly believed in. But passion doesn't pay the bills—or help me grow into the lifestyle I envisioned for myself. After watching one of my favorite Alux YouTube videos on negotiating a raise, I felt inspired.

The video made it seem straightforward: gather your achievements, build a solid case, and go for it. The worst they can say is no, right? With that thought fueling my courage, I requested a meeting with my boss.

Sitting across from them, I laid out everything I'd accomplished: improvements in team efficiency, successful projects, and the countless late nights ensuring our programs thrived. They nodded thoughtfully, gave me a faint smile, and said, "We'll consider it."

"Consider" was corporate speak for "not going to happen," but at least I tried. That attempt planted a seed, though. As much as I loved the mission of my job, it was becoming clear that my time there might be nearing its end. If growth wasn't an option here, I needed to look elsewhere.

For months, I quietly explored project manager roles, casting my net far and wide. I had no ties keeping me in my current city, so I decided: why not start fresh? New York City stood out as my dream destination. I'd visited the city before, and its relentless energy called to me like no other place. But the competition was fierce, and I wasn't above starting somewhere else if the opportunity was right.

While navigating this transitional period, I was determined to maintain my independence. No handouts, no shortcuts—just hard work and resilience. Traveling became my outlet. It was during a summer trip to NYC for World Pride that I rekindled my love for the city. The vibrant streets, the diverse people, the limitless possibilities—I couldn't resist coming back.

When Christmas rolled around, I made plans to return. This time, I'd experience NYC in the winter, a whole new adventure. I reached out to my friends Yogi and Chester, and before I knew it, my flight was booked.

The moment I stepped off the plane, the winter chill hit me like a freight train. Within minutes, my face felt frozen, but I couldn't help smiling. This was the magic of New York. I hopped on the Q bus to meet Yogi and his godfather Gary. We spent the afternoon catching up over diner food, sharing laughs, and planning the week ahead.

"Christopher Street bars are a must," Yogi said, his eyes lighting up. "And dancing! You need to let loose."

I was all for it. With some time to spare, I visited my brother and his family before Yogi swung by to pick me up. After introductions and a quick exchange of pleasantries, we dove into the night's adventures.

Christopher Street was alive with energy, even in the frigid cold. We hopped from bar to bar, each stop filled with laughter, great music, and unforgettable moments. By the time we reached the final club, I was in my element, surrounded by good friends and a city I adored.

It was Latin Night, and the music was infectious. I found myself on the dance floor, moving to the rhythm, lost in the moment. That's when he appeared—a tall, confident man with a warm smile. He started dancing with me, but I was too engrossed in my solo groove to fully engage. After a few moments, I politely stepped away, retreating into my thoughts.

The night continued, and as the DJ played the last songs, the lights came on. Yogi and Gary were ready for food, and accompanying them were two newcomers: Danny and Manny. Manny's face was familiar—it was the man who had approached me on the dance floor.

Introductions were quick. "This is Danny," Yogi said, gesturing to the bald gentleman, "and this is Manny."

"Nice to meet you," I said, offering a polite smile. But food was the priority.

Yogi and Gary left it to me to choose a spot, and out of all the options in NYC, I opted for classic fast food. We settled into a booth, but with the limited space, I chose to sit alone at a high-top table. Moments later, Manny joined me.

"Why don't you sit with Danny and them?" I asked, half-joking, half-serious.

"I'm fine here," he replied casually, settling in with his tray.

I decided to let it go, and before long, we fell into a surprisingly engaging conversation. His tattoos caught my attention first—anime characters I recognized. Complimenting them was an easy icebreaker, and from there, the dialogue flowed naturally.

We talked about work, discovering striking similarities in our paths. Manny was pursuing a master's degree while teaching at a dual-language school for children with special needs. His dedication was inspiring, and the way he spoke about his students showed genuine passion.

"What made you choose that path?" I asked, leaning in, captivated.

"My mom," he said softly. "She always taught me the value of helping others, and working with kids just felt right. They remind me of how important it is to see the world differently."

His words resonated deeply. We shared stories of our struggles and goals, finding common ground in our ambitions and nerdy interests. I felt a pang of guilt for dismissing him earlier on the dance floor. He was smart, kind, and undeniably beautiful.

After finishing our meals, the group began to head out. Yogi, Gary, and Danny walked ahead, leaving Manny and me trailing behind. Our conversation continued effortlessly, the cold air biting at our faces but failing to dampen the connection growing between us.

Before parting ways, Manny hesitated. "Can I get your Instagram?" he asked.

I laughed, shaking my head. "How about we exchange numbers instead? We'd just end up asking for them later."

He chuckled, pulling out his phone. We swapped numbers, and as he turned to join Danny, he paused. Without overthinking, I leaned in, and we shared a kiss—soft, electric, and full of promise.

As I watched him walk away, a warmth spread through me, cutting through the winter chill. That spark, so unexpected yet undeniable, felt like the start of something extraordinary.

The next morning, I woke up to the soft vibration of my phone on the nightstand. It was Manny. Just seeing his name on the screen sent a rush of excitement through me, the kind of excitement I hadn't felt in a long time. We began texting back and forth, first exchanging small talk about how cold it was outside and how late the night had gone. But soon, our conversation took a deeper turn.

I was beginning to realize just how much of a crush I had on him. There was something about Manny that felt different—authentic. The way he carried himself, his calm confidence, and the genuine kindness he exuded had me hooked.

Even though I was anxious to see him again, I didn't want to come across as too eager. I tried to keep things casual, but every time my phone buzzed with his message, my heart leapt. Finally, he suggested we meet up later that day.

"I'd love to," I replied, probably too quickly. But I didn't care. My time in NYC was limited, and I wanted to make the most of it.

By the afternoon, I was bundled up in my coat, navigating the subway like a pro—or at least trying to. I was heading to meet Manny, and my heart was racing the entire ride. As the train screeched to a stop, I stepped out and walked toward the store where we had agreed to meet.

I stood there, hands stuffed into my coat pockets, my breath visible in the frigid air. I kept checking my phone, trying not to seem too nervous. Finally, I looked up and spotted him crossing the street.

There he was, his frame tall and confident, his smile warm despite the icy chill. Watching him approach, I felt an inexplicable joy bubbling up inside me, like a dog wagging its tail uncontrollably. What was this feeling?

"Hey," Manny greeted me with a smile that could melt even the coldest day.

"Hey," I managed, suddenly shy. We hugged briefly, the kind of hug that made me want to linger just a moment longer.

"Ready to seize the day?" he asked, his enthusiasm contagious.

"Absolutely," I said, and we set off on what would become one of the most memorable days of my life.

Our first stop was The Strand, the famous bookstore. The warmth inside was a welcome contrast to the biting cold outside. Rows upon rows of books surrounded us, the scent of old pages filling the air.

"You into reading?" Manny asked as we wandered through the aisles.

"Definitely," I said, running my fingers along the spines of books. "It's like getting lost in a different world. What about you?"

"I love it," he admitted. "It's why I want to write a children's book one day. Something that inspires kids the way books inspired me when I was younger."

"That's amazing," I said, genuinely impressed.

We talked about our favorite books and stories, sharing laughs over some of the more embarrassing titles we'd read in our teens. The conversation flowed so naturally, it felt like we'd known each other forever.

Afterward, we found a cozy little café and ordered steaming bowls of soup to warm up. As we sat by the window, watching the bustling city outside, our conversation turned more personal.

"So, what made you decide to work with kids?" I asked, curious.

Manny's face softened. "It's a long story," he began. "But the short version is, I had a teacher who believed in me when no one else did. I wanted to be that person for someone else."

"That's... really beautiful," I said, feeling a pang of admiration.

"What about you?" he asked. "What drives you?"

I hesitated for a moment before replying. "Honestly, I want to prove to myself that I can make something of my life. I don't want handouts. I want to build my life from the ground up."

Manny nodded, his eyes thoughtful. "I get that. There's something empowering about knowing you earned everything you have."

As the day wore on, neither of us seemed ready to say goodbye. We tossed around the idea of splitting a hotel room so we could spend more time together. The idea seemed spontaneous but exciting.

The hotel we chose was stunning—modern, sleek, with a definite millennial vibe. We met at the bar downstairs, where we continued talking over drinks.

"I'm glad we did this," I said, raising my glass to him.

"Me too," Manny said, clinking his glass against mine. "This day's been... special."

I could feel the sincerity in his words, and it made my heart flutter.

Later, my cousin reached out to invite me to a late Christmas dinner in Long Island. Without thinking, I asked Manny if he wanted to come along.

"Are you sure?" he asked, looking a bit hesitant.

"Absolutely," I said. "They'll love you."

The drive to Long Island felt like stepping into a quieter world, away from the rush of Manhattan. Manny sat beside me, a quiet confidence in his demeanor. I occasionally glanced at him, feeling a mix of nerves and excitement about introducing him to my family.

"So," he said, breaking the silence, "what's the family like?"

"They're loud, nosy, and completely overwhelming," I admitted with a laugh. "But they're also loving and have no filter. Consider yourself warned."

"I'll survive," he said with a wink.

When we arrived, my cousin greeted us with a warm hug. The house smelled like roasted meat and spices, and the sound of laughter echoed from the kitchen. Manny offered a charming smile as I introduced him to everyone.

"This is Manny," I said, trying to keep my voice casual.

"Nice to meet you all," he said, holding out his hand.

My aunt, always the bold one, bypassed the handshake and pulled him into a hug. "Manny, huh? We'll see if you pass the test," she teased, giving me a sly smile.

The evening unfolded like a scene from a holiday movie. Plates of food passed around the table, stories shared, and Manny handled every curveball my family threw at him with grace.

It wasn't until dessert that the infamous milk moment happened.

"What can I get you to drink?" my cousin asked.

"Milk, if you have it," Manny replied without hesitation.

The room fell silent. Every face turned toward him in unison, and then the laughter erupted.

"Milk?" my uncle said, shaking his head. "You're something else."

"To each their own," Manny said with a grin, holding his ground.

The moment became an instant family joke, one that Manny leaned into for the rest of the evening.

When it was time to leave, my family surprised me by giving Manny a warm goodbye hug. As we walked back to the car, he looked over at me.

"That wasn't so bad," he said.

"They love you," I replied.

"And the milk?" he teased.

"They'll never let it go," I laughed.

When New Year's Eve rolled around, Yogi invited everyone to his mom's apartment. I asked if I could bring Manny, and Yogi welcomed the idea without hesitation.

Yogi's mom's apartment was already buzzing with energy when I arrived. The space was warm and welcoming, filled with the smell of home-cooked food and the sound of salsa music playing in the background.

Manny arrived a little later, his arms filled with a box of baked goods. When he stepped through the door, Yogi's mom lit up.

"Who's this handsome young man?" she asked, pulling him into a hug before he could even respond.

"Manny," I said, grinning.

"He brought dessert!" she exclaimed, taking the box from his hands and leading him to the kitchen.

The apartment was filled with Yogi's extended family, most of whom were speaking rapid-fire Spanish. Manny fit in effortlessly, laughing and nodding along even when he didn't understand every word.

At one point, I caught Yogi's mom chatting with Manny at the dining table. Her eyes lit up every time he spoke, and it was clear she was smitten.

"Yogi," she whispered loudly enough for me to hear. "This one's a keeper."

Yogi smirked and leaned toward me. "She thinks Manny's here with me."

"Let's keep it that way," I said, stifling a laugh.

As the evening wore on, I found myself standing next to Manny by the window, looking out at the twinkling city lights.

"Feels like the year's ending on a high note," I said softly.

"It really does," he replied, his voice steady.

When the countdown began, the room erupted in cheers and anticipation. At the stroke of midnight, Manny turned to me. Without hesitation, he leaned in, and we shared a kiss that felt like the perfect start to the new year.

Yogi's mom, who had been watching, turned to Yogi with wide eyes.

"Wait," she said, utterly confused. "I thought he was here with you!"

Yogi threw his hands up, laughing. "I never said that!"

The whole room burst into laughter, and I couldn't stop smiling. The night ended with hugs, cheers, and Manny holding my hand as we welcomed the new year together.

The next evening, the inevitable moment came. My suitcase sat by the door, a stark reminder that my time in New York was coming to an end. Manny met me at the subway station, and the weight of the goodbye hung in the air between us.

"Feels like the week flew by," I said, trying to keep my voice light.

"It did," he agreed, his hands in his pockets. "Too fast."

For a moment, we stood in silence, the noise of the city around us. I felt a lump rise in my throat, but I swallowed it down.

"I'm going to miss this," I admitted softly.

"You don't have to," he said, his eyes meeting mine. "I meant what I said—I'll come visit. You just say the word."

"Really?" I asked, a spark of hope in my voice.

"Of course," he replied, his tone firm. "This... this doesn't feel like something that should end here."

I nodded, feeling a mixture of sadness and excitement.

"I'll hold you to that," I said, trying to smile.

"You'd better," he teased, leaning in for a kiss.

As the train approached, I felt a wave of emotions wash over me. I stepped inside and turned to see him standing there, his hands in his pockets, a small smile on his face.

The doors closed, and the train began to move, but I kept my eyes on him until he was out of sight.

As I settled into my seat, I couldn't help but smile. I didn't know what the future held, but for the first time in a long time, I felt like I had something to look forward to—and that something was Manny.

Manny and I couldn't go a day without talking. Every text, every FaceTime call, made the miles between us feel just a little shorter.

"Alright, King," Manny said one night over FaceTime, his smile lighting up the screen. "If I'm flying all the way down to Florida, you'd better impress me. What's on the itinerary?"

"Lake Harmony, my favorite taco spot, and... well, you'll just have to wait for the last one."

"Why do you always have to be so mysterious?" he teased, rolling his eyes dramatically.

"Because you love it."

He laughed, but his expression softened. "You know, I really do."

We FaceTimed often, even sneaking calls during work breaks. Manny taught kindergarten, and I loved hearing him gush about his students.

"Today, one of my kids told me I'm their favorite queen in the world," he said one afternoon, his voice warm with pride.

"They're not wrong," I replied.

As February approached, we made plans for his visit. Since I was renting a room from my friend Louie, having guests over wasn't an option. Manny booked a hotel without hesitation.

"It's just a place to sleep," he said. "The rest of the time, I'll be with you."

I couldn't let Valentine's Day pass without doing something special. I mailed him a box filled with his favorite anime cards, candy, and tiny dinosaur finger puppets for his students.

When he got the package, he called immediately. "Are you serious right now? This is the cutest thing anyone's ever done for me!"

"You deserve it," I said. "And I thought the kids would like the dinosaurs."

"Like them? They're gonna lose their minds!" Manny laughed, holding up the puppets. "You're such a sweetheart, you know that?"

The weekend of Manny's visit finally arrived. When I saw him at the airport, my heart skipped a beat. He looked radiant—his confidence, his presence, everything about him commanded attention.

"There's my King," he said, pulling me into a hug.

"And there's my Queen," I replied, grinning.

The weekend was perfect. We walked around the lake, ate at my favorite spots, and laughed until our cheeks hurt. He met some of my friends over dinner, charming them effortlessly.

"So, how'd you manage to snag someone as fabulous as Manny?" one of my friends asked me.

"I just got lucky," I said, and I meant it.

After he left, we made plans for me to visit him in March. Manny lived in Queens, and I was excited to see the city through his eyes.

"I can't wait to show you around," he said over the phone. "You're gonna fall in love with New York all over again."

"I think I already have," I replied.

I also shared some exciting news. "I've got an interview for a Project Manager role at a cancer hospital in Manhattan."

"Shut up! That's amazing!" Manny exclaimed. "You'd kill it in that role— and it'd bring you closer to me."

"That's the plan," I said, already imagining a future where we didn't have to count down the days between visits.

When March came, I flew to New York. The city felt different—quieter, more subdued.

"This virus is messing everything up," Manny said as we walked through his neighborhood.

"It's eerie," I agreed, noting the shuttered shops and sparse crowds.

We spent most of our time indoors, sharing meals and watching movies. Despite the strange circumstances, being with Manny made everything feel right.

But the weekend flew by, and as soon as I landed back in Florida, the borders closed, and travel was halted.

When the pandemic hit, everything changed, and it forced Manny and me to adapt quickly. The excitement and anticipation we once felt about seeing each other in person turned into long-distance relationship challenges. But we were committed to making it work, even if the circumstances were far from ideal.

We turned to technology to bridge the gap—endless FaceTime calls, even on workdays when I'd sneak a call during a lunch break or when Manny had a rare free moment between teaching. We kept each other entertained, distracted from the chaos unfolding in the world outside. But despite all the effort we put into staying connected, the strain of being physically apart was starting to show.

I remember one night, we did one of our "movie nights." We'd pick a movie at random on Netflix, and then we'd start it at the same time. The idea was that we could share the experience in real time, even if we weren't in the same room. Manny picked The Old Guard, and we spent the next two hours texting each other sarcastic commentary.

"That's gonna be me when I'm 300 years old," I joked, sending him a message.

"Yeah, but you'd be the first to get yourself killed," Manny replied.

We laughed, but as the days and weeks dragged on, I could sense a quiet tension creeping in. I knew that the uncertainty of the world and the isolation were weighing heavily on both of us. The excitement of our surprise food deliveries—the sushi he sent me one night, and the Thai food I sent him another—slowly faded into routine. The fun, playful spirit we once had began to feel a little... forced.

Then, in an unexpected twist, I received the email from the cancer hospital in Manhattan. They were retracting the Project Manager position due to the pandemic's economic impact. The opportunity I'd been working so hard for evaporated just like that. I tried not to let it affect me too much, but it was one more blow in a year already full of them. Manny, ever the optimist, reassured me.

"Don't let this setback define you. You're still going to land something amazing," he said during one of our calls. But even though he was supportive, I could feel him withdrawing. Something was changing in him.

It wasn't sudden—it had been building for weeks. The communication started to shift from daily check-ins to a few messages here and there. When we did speak, it felt like we were grasping for something that was slipping away, but neither of us wanted to admit it.

One afternoon, I finally felt the tension reach its breaking point. We had a phone conversation, and I could hear it in his voice—something was wrong.

"I can't do this anymore," Manny said quietly, the words hanging in the air between us.

"Do what? Us?" I asked, my heart sinking in my chest.

He sighed deeply. "I don't know if I'm ready for this, for anything right now. I've been rushing through relationships, not giving myself time to heal, and I need space to figure it all out."

His words hit like a brick wall. I wanted to scream, to demand answers, but I could hear the sincerity in his voice. This wasn't about me. He wasn't rejecting me; he was rejecting himself. And yet, it still stung.

"I get it," I said, though I didn't entirely understand. "But this sucks, Manny. I can't keep pretending everything's fine."

"I know," he replied, his voice tinged with regret. "It's just... I don't know who I am right now. I need to figure that out."

And just like that, the connection we'd fought so hard to build began to unravel.

For weeks, I felt paralyzed. There was no closure, no explanation that felt satisfying. We agreed to cut off contact, thinking that it was better that way. I went into survival mode—burying myself in work, in my personal goals, trying to fill the void he'd left behind. But the truth was, I missed him more than I cared to admit.

The days after the breakup were a blur. Some moments, I would be a mess—crying uncontrollably in bed, mourning the loss of a relationship I thought had real potential. Then, out of nowhere, I'd feel this surge of anger. I threw a pillow across the room in frustration, followed by a string of curse words at the empty walls.

The swings between sorrow and rage were exhausting. I knew I couldn't keep it up forever, so I did the one thing I knew would help—reached out for help. I scheduled an appointment with Dr. Hill, my therapist, who had helped me in the past. The first session was brutal. I cried through most of it, talking about how the relationship had unraveled.

"I don't even know why I'm angry," I told Dr. Hill. "He wasn't wrong for doing what he did. He needed to find himself. But it still hurts. And I feel like I've lost something that mattered so much to me."

Dr. Hill nodded. "It's okay to feel hurt. Sometimes, we hold onto things we don't fully understand because they feel like part of us. But healing doesn't happen overnight."

It was a long process, but slowly, I began to gain clarity. I spent time reflecting on my own journey—how far I'd come after my previous heartbreak with Roberto and how much I'd learned about myself. I realized that while Manny was important to me, I had to focus on myself first. I was no longer going to let his actions define my worth.

I knew I needed closure, though. Not just for the relationship, but for my own peace of mind.

By Thanksgiving, travel restrictions had eased, and I felt a renewed sense of courage. I was going back to New York, and this time, I knew I had to face Manny, if only to clear the air.

I reached out to him, expecting nothing but an awkward exchange. Instead, he agreed to meet for dinner.

The moment I saw him, my heart raced. His presence was just as magnetic as ever, but something was different now. He looked at me, not with the uncertainty I'd seen in his eyes months ago, but with a quiet understanding.

At dinner, we bantered, the old playful tension between us still present, though less intense. I even wore the jacket he'd mailed back to me, just to tease him.

"Nice jacket," Manny remarked dryly, though I could sense the faintest smile tugging at his lips.

I decided to be honest—something I hadn't done with him before. "Have you found yourself yet?" I asked, my voice a mix of sarcasm and curiosity.

"Still searching," he replied, his tone matching mine.

As the dinner progressed, we eased into a more civil conversation. Manny turned to me and apologized for how things ended. He acknowledged that he could've handled it better.

"I'm sorry for shutting you out," he admitted. "You deserved better."

I didn't hold back. "You're right," I said, my voice firm but not angry. "I didn't deserve that." It felt good to say it—to finally give myself the respect I deserved.

We parted that night with a hug, and for the first time in months, I felt a sense of closure. We may not have been right for each other, but we'd grown. And that was enough for me.

Manny and I still keep in touch occasionally—more through social media than actual conversations—but I can't help but feel a sense of pride as I watch him thrive. He's still my Queen, in my heart. But I've learned that life has a funny way of leading us down paths we never expect.

Maybe Manny was the one that got away. Maybe not. But I know that our time together was significant.

In the end, we were both on our own journeys—he, trying to figure out his next chapter, and me, learning how to stand on my own. If our paths cross again in the future, maybe it will be as something more. Or maybe it will just be a moment in time we'll remember fondly.

For now, I take comfort in knowing that Manny made a lasting, positive impact on my life. And that, in itself, is enough.

Transformative

Life moved forward, albeit at a pace that felt slow and weighed down by monotony. Each morning I woke up, poured myself into my nonprofit work, and repeated the cycle. Though some restrictions had been lifted post-pandemic, I was grateful that we could still work from home. The steady rhythm of my work gave me a purpose, but I couldn't shake the persistent feeling of being stuck. Every day felt like a balancing act between doing the job I once loved and planning for my next big step.

By the summer of 2021, that feeling boiled over into action. Three years with the nonprofit had brought many lessons but no financial growth. Promotions were nearly impossible in such a small organization, and any hope of upward mobility had long since fizzled. In a desperate attempt to prove my worth, I even proposed taking on more responsibility for the same pay. Surely, any company would jump at the chance for extra work without an additional cost. But leadership, detached and uninspired, dismissed the idea.

That was the breaking point. Leadership's lack of passion mirrored the stagnation I felt in my role. I couldn't make a positive impact if those at the helm weren't as invested as I was. It became painfully clear that I needed to leave, and so I cast my net wide, applying for project management positions across the country—from California to Minnesota, New York to Virginia. I even applied to roles in my hometown, hoping for something to reignite my career.

The job hunt was a whirlwind of interviews. Opportunities came and went, but none seemed like the perfect fit. Some positions offered excellent pay but were in cities with living costs so high they negated the salary bump. Then, a nonprofit in Boston caught my attention. Their mission was unique—volunteers went into public schools in struggling neighborhoods to teach children games during recess. The program used play not just as a means of entertainment but as a way to teach conflict resolution and promote emotional growth. It was beautiful, the kind of work I could throw my heart into.

The interview process was long and rigorous, stretching over three months and involving three interviews, reference checks, and hours of preparation. Finally, I got the call with the job offer. I should have felt elated, but the timing complicated things. Just three days prior, I'd received another offer—this time from a local hospital for a position as a front desk associate in pediatrics. The pay was slightly less than what I earned at the nonprofit, but the potential for growth made it a promising choice.

The decision weighed heavily on me. The Boston job offered a change of scenery and an exciting mission, but the salary barely covered basic living expenses. The hospital job, though not glamorous, felt stable and offered room for upward mobility. After hours of deliberation, pros-and-cons lists, and late-night research, I chose the hospital. It wasn't the more exciting option, but it felt like the smarter move.

The hospital welcomed me with open arms. From day one, I made it clear I wasn't there to coast—I had goals and wasn't willing to remain stagnant. To my surprise, the hospital offered extra hours in the ICU helping with COVID patients. The risk was palpable, but so was the financial reward. My checks doubled, allowing me to finally feel some financial relief.

Working in pediatrics was surprisingly fun. I clicked with my coworkers quickly, forming friendships that made each day enjoyable. By the fifth month, I'd already set my sights on a promotion, and my boss noticed my drive. When the six-month mark hit, I earned a promotion to front desk supervisor at one of the largest hospital locations. The transition was bittersweet—I'd grown close to my pediatric team—but they encouraged me to keep pushing forward.

Fate had another surprise in store. My new location placed me just one floor above Chelsea, a college friend. Though we had kept in touch over

the years—sharing stories, occasional trips, and updates on life—
working in the same building brought us closer than ever.

Chelsea and I quickly fell into a routine of lunch breaks and after-work
chats. Inevitably, the topic of dating came up. Since Manny, my love life
had been a series of dead ends. Conversations on dating apps often felt
like pulling teeth, and most of the men I met seemed focused on short-
term gratification. It wasn't my style. I craved genuine emotional
connection, the kind that made you feel seen and valued. Unfortunately,
it seemed like an outdated concept in the modern dating world.

Men on the apps often had profiles advertising "open relationships,"
something I respected but didn't personally resonate with. Monogamy
felt right for me, and while I admired the trust and communication
required for open dynamics, I knew where my comfort zone lay. After
months of frustration, I decided to take a break from dating apps and
focus on myself.

During this time, I poured energy into my relationships with family and
friends. Inspired by a Kurzgesagt video about life's fleeting nature, I
began calling my parents daily. Each conversation was a reminder of the
importance of cherishing the connections that truly mattered.

After a few months, Chelsea encouraged me to give dating apps another
shot. "Not every guy is a dud," she teased over coffee. Reluctantly, I
reactivated my profile on one app. To my surprise, I found a message
from Joey, an incredibly attractive man whose profile seemed too good
to be true. He had messaged me four months earlier. Figuring I had
nothing to lose, I replied.

I wasn't expecting much—surely he had moved on by now. But to my
shock, he responded two weeks later.

Growth

The conversations with Joey began like most on a dating app—brief and cautious. But there was something about him that made me want to keep talking. After a bit of back-and-forth, I decided to address the obvious.

"Hey, so... I feel like I owe you an apology for replying so late," I wrote. "I've been off the app for a few months, trying to take a break from everything."

His response came quickly, much to my surprise. "No worries at all," he said. "I get it. I'm on and off here too. It's tough finding someone who's actually looking for something meaningful."

That comment struck a chord with me. I had been feeling the exact same way.

Our conversation flowed naturally after that. Joey shared that he was currently out of the country visiting family, which immediately gave me pause.

"Where are you right now?" I asked, trying to sound casual but dreading the answer.

"In the UK," he said.

I couldn't help but sigh internally. "Of course," I thought. "This ridiculously attractive guy probably lives thousands of miles away."

Sensing my concern, Joey quickly clarified. "But I live near you, actually. I just like to work remotely and travel when I can."

"You work remotely?" I replied, my envy spilling over into my words. "That's such an amazing setup. I'm jealous!"

He laughed, sending a string of laughing emojis in return. "It's not bad. Gives me the freedom to explore and stay with family when I want."

The conversation soon turned to his profile pictures.

"Okay, I have to ask," I typed, hesitating for a moment. "Are these pictures really you? Because they look... professional."

Joey responded with good humor. "They are. My sister's a photographer and did a photoshoot for me. She said I needed to show myself off more. It was her way of building my confidence."

"That's actually really sweet of her," I replied, feeling a new layer of admiration for him.

After a week of chatting, we decided to exchange numbers. Our first phone call lasted over two hours, and we talked about everything—our childhoods, what had brought us to this point in life, and why we were still single.

Joey opened up about his past relationship. "I was with my ex-husband for nine years," he said, his voice soft. "We were married for four of those. Things just... didn't work out."

I hesitated for a moment before asking the question that had been lingering in my mind. "Do you feel like you're ready to date again? I just... don't want either of us wasting time if you're still processing things."

He didn't miss a beat. "I appreciate you asking that," he said. "But yes, I'm ready to move forward. I wouldn't be here otherwise."

His answer reassured me, and our conversations continued, each one delving deeper than the last. He'd send me videos of the beautiful countryside in the UK, and I'd share pictures of my favorite art pieces, knowing how much he loved creativity.

Finally, after weeks of talking, we made plans to meet when he returned.

The day of our date arrived, and my nerves were a mix of excitement and anxiety. I had spent the morning picking out the perfect outfit, finally settling on a fitted red shirt. There was something about wearing red—it made me feel bold and confident, even if I wasn't entirely sure I would need the boost.

As I pulled up to the restaurant, I spotted Joey stepping out of his car. For a moment, I just sat there, taking him in. He looked exactly like his pictures, only better. He was shorter than me, which was endearing, with smooth skin and a red beanie perched perfectly on his head. His smile—bright, warm, and framed by perfect teeth—was disarming.

"Hey!" he called out, his voice cheerful as he approached me.

"Hi," I managed, stepping out of my car. I was caught off guard by how naturally good-looking he was in person. We hugged briefly, and even in that small gesture, I felt a sense of comfort.

Inside the restaurant, we were greeted by the cozy hum of quiet conversations and the faint aroma of spices. It was an intimate little place with lanterns hanging from the ceiling and a wall of handwritten notes from past diners.

Joey immediately complimented the choice of venue. "This is such a cool spot," he said, glancing around.

"Glad you like it," I replied. "It's one of my favorite hidden gems."

We settled into a corner booth, and the conversation picked up as naturally as it had over the phone. Joey had an effortless charm—he made me laugh with his dry humor and witty remarks about the quirks of living abroad.

When the food arrived, we both shared bites of our dishes, joking about how adventurous—or not—we were with trying new flavors.

"You're braver than I thought," he teased as I tried a particularly spicy dish he ordered.

"Don't underestimate me," I shot back, earning one of his signature grins.

After we finished eating, neither of us seemed ready to end the date. "Want to walk around a bit?" I suggested.

"I'd love to," Joey replied without hesitation.

We wandered into the nearby downtown area, where the streets were lined with boutiques, cafes, and small art galleries. I led him to a local museum I loved, a quaint place with a mix of historical artifacts and modern art.

"This is one of my favorite spots," I told him as we entered.

"Lead the way," he said, clearly intrigued.

Joey was fascinated by everything. His eyes lingered on each piece, and he asked thoughtful questions that made me appreciate the art in new ways. At one point, he stopped in front of a sculpture—a modern, abstract piece with sharp angles and fluid curves.

"This one's incredible," he said, his voice almost reverent. "It feels like it's alive, like it's still moving."

His passion was contagious, and I found myself drawn to the piece in a way I hadn't been before. "I've never looked at it like that," I admitted.

Outside, as we stepped back into the fresh air, the sky suddenly darkened, and raindrops began to fall.

"Looks like we're getting caught in it," Joey said, laughing as he pulled his beanie tighter over his head.

"Wait here," I said, already running toward the parking lot.

"Are you sure?" he called after me, his laughter echoing in the rain.

By the time I reached my car and drove back to him, I was completely drenched. Water dripped from my hair, and my shirt clung to me like a second skin.

Joey's expression was a mix of amusement and admiration. "You're a hero," he said, handing me a napkin he'd grabbed from the museum's front desk.

"I try," I replied, wringing out my hair and shaking water off my arms.

The rain didn't dampen our spirits; if anything, it added a layer of spontaneity to the day. We ended up at a cozy coffee shop, sitting in a corner booth with steaming mugs of chai lattes.

Time seemed to stand still as we talked. Joey had this way of making me feel like the only person in the room, completely focused and engaged. We laughed over silly anecdotes, shared deeper stories about our lives, and debated which Harry Potter house we'd belong to.

Hours passed, and it wasn't until a barista came by to politely inform us that they were closing that we realized how late it had gotten.

"I guess we've been here a while," Joey said, glancing at his watch with a sheepish grin.

"Time flies when the company's good," I replied, smiling back.

Outside, the air was cool and damp, the rain having tapered off into a gentle mist. I drove Joey back to his car, neither of us wanting to end the night but knowing we had to.

As we stood by his car, he turned to me with that bright smile that had disarmed me all day.

"Thanks for today," he said softly.

"Thank you," I replied. "I had an amazing time."

We hugged briefly, the moment charged with unspoken possibilities.

As I drove home, I couldn't help but replay the day in my mind. It felt like the beginning of something special, and for the first time in a long time, I allowed myself to hope.

The days with Joey turned into weeks, and weeks turned into months. The more time we spent together, the more I found myself going above and beyond to make him happy. It wasn't a chore—it felt natural, almost instinctive. I'd surprise him with flowers, open doors for him, and plan dates that ranged from intimate dinners at home to spontaneous road trips to nearby cities. For me, these gestures felt like second nature, but Joey reacted as if I'd hung the moon.

"You always do the sweetest things," he said one evening as I handed him a bouquet of his favorite flowers.

"It's nothing," I replied, brushing it off with a smile. "You deserve it."

A few months in, Joey shared something weighing on him: his mother might move in with him.

"It's just a possibility for now," he explained over dinner. "She's been going through a rough patch, and I want to help."

As a self-proclaimed mama's boy, I could understand his instinct to care for her. Still, I couldn't help but think about the privacy we'd lose.

"I get it," I said after a pause. "Family comes first. But... what about your siblings? Couldn't they help out?"

Joey shook his head. "They all have kids and families of their own. I'm the only one with the space and flexibility."

I nodded, trying to hide my selfish concern. His home—a place he'd once shared with his ex-husband—was now his own. While my place was shared with a roommate, Joey lived alone, making it the natural choice for his mother. I didn't voice my worry about how it might impact us, knowing it wasn't my decision to make.

"Whatever you decide, I'll support you," I said, reaching for his hand.

Joey smiled, his eyes soft with gratitude. "Thank you. That means a lot."

It was around this time—three months into dating—that Joey brought up a question I'd been avoiding.

"So, why aren't we calling each other boyfriends yet?" he asked one night as we lounged on the couch, his head resting on my shoulder.

I froze, unsure how to answer. "I... I guess I'm just taking my time," I admitted. "We're exclusive, and things are great, but I don't feel the need to rush into a title."

Joey sat up, frowning slightly. "I don't understand. If we're exclusive and we're happy, what's the harm in calling it what it is?"

"It's not about harm," I said carefully. "It's about being sure. We're still getting to know each other, and I just want to make sure this is right before we label it."

He looked at me with an intensity that made me squirm. "Are you sure this isn't about wanting to keep your options open?"

The accusation stung. "That's not it at all," I said firmly. "I've been focusing on you. I even deleted my dating profile after our second date because I knew I wanted to give this a real chance."

Joey's expression softened, but he didn't let up. "Then why not make it official? It feels like you're holding back."

I sighed, running a hand through my hair. "I am holding back," I admitted. "But it's not because I don't care about you. It's because I've been hurt before, and I'm scared of diving in too quickly and ending up in the same place."

We went back and forth for what felt like an eternity. Joey's persistence was unwavering, and eventually, I caved.

"Fine," I said with a sigh. "We can call each other boyfriends."

Joey beamed, pulling me into a tight hug. "You won't regret this, I promise."

But as I held him, a part of me felt uneasy. It wasn't that I didn't care about Joey—I did. But I couldn't shake the feeling that I'd been pressured into making a decision before I was ready.

As our relationship continued, Joey began to open up more about his past. He told me about his ex-husband—a man who, from Joey's descriptions, hadn't been the best fit for him.

"I think I was just so focused on making it work that I didn't see how unhappy we both were," Joey admitted one evening.

"Why didn't you end it?" I asked gently.

Joey hesitated, his gaze dropping to his hands. "It's hard to explain. My religion played a big part in it. I felt... bound, like I had to make it work no matter what."

His words sparked a flicker of concern in me. If he'd stayed in an unhealthy marriage out of obligation, what did that mean for us? Would he expect the same unwavering commitment from me, even if things went south?

I pushed the thought aside, focusing instead on reassuring him. "You don't have to prove anything to anyone, Joey," I said. "You deserve to be happy."

He smiled, but the conversation left me with more questions than answers.

Despite my lingering doubts, I made an effort to show Joey how much I cared. I paid close attention to his love languages—words of affirmation and physical touch.

"You're amazing, you know that?" I told him one night as we curled up on the couch.

"Coming from you, that means everything," he replied, his voice soft.

I made a point to hold his hand, kiss his forehead, and remind him daily that he was the only person I was focusing on.

For now, it seemed like enough. But deep down, I knew there were still hurdles we'd have to face—his past, my fears, and the uncertainty of what lay ahead.

The shift in our relationship began just before my 31st birthday. It wasn't something I planned or expected—it just unfolded, one decision, one moment, at a time.

An old friend of mine reached out with an incredible offer: a week-long luxury cruise for next to nothing. My friend worked on the ship and had access to discounted guest passes. It was an opportunity I couldn't pass up.

"Wow," Joey said when I told him about it over dinner. "That sounds amazing. Can I come too?"

I hesitated. "It's not that simple. My friend has a limited number of people he can invite. But I'll ask and see what I can do, okay?"

Joey nodded, but I could tell he wasn't completely satisfied with my answer.

A few days passed, and before I could reach out to my friend with a proper request, Joey had already made his move.

"I figured it out!" he announced, practically buzzing with excitement.

"Figured what out?"

"The cruise," he said. "I did some research. I can get my own cabin, I've calculated the cost, and I even got my PTO approved!"

I blinked, caught off guard. "Joey... I hadn't even had the chance to ask yet. My friend doesn't know you, and I didn't want to push him before understanding all the details."

Joey's enthusiasm dimmed slightly. "I just thought this way, it'd be less of a burden for him if I handled my own arrangements."

"It's not about the logistics," I explained, trying to soften the blow. "It's about respecting the boundaries of the invitation."

Eventually, I did speak to my friend. While hesitant, he managed to secure Joey a spot on the trip. We went together, but the situation added a subtle strain.

The cruise itself was breathtaking—something out of a dream. The ship sparkled under the sunlight as it glided across the endless turquoise waves. Each day was packed with activities, gourmet meals, and stunning views. It should have been perfect, but the tension simmering beneath the surface between Joey, my friend, and me added an unexpected weight.

Joey was excited, perhaps too excited. He wanted to be included in every conversation, every plan, every moment. My friend, however, wasn't as warm or inviting. He had a sharp, no-nonsense personality that could be difficult to navigate, especially for someone as sensitive as Joey.

One evening, Joey and I sat on the upper deck, watching the sun melt into the horizon, painting the ocean in hues of gold and orange. Joey broke the silence.

"Your friend doesn't like me," he said, staring at the water.

I sighed, already anticipating this conversation. "Joey, that's not true. He's just... tough to get to know. He's been through a lot, and sometimes it takes time for him to warm up to people."

Joey shook his head. "It feels like every time I try to talk to him, he gives me short answers or looks at me like I'm in the way."

"Maybe you're overthinking it," I offered gently. "He's not the easiest person to read, but it doesn't mean he dislikes you."

"It's more than that," Joey insisted. "I feel like I'm intruding on something. Like I'm the third wheel on this trip."

His words stung, not because they were completely untrue, but because I didn't know how to bridge the gap between them. Joey's discomfort was palpable, and I felt caught in the middle—trying to enjoy the trip while also managing their conflicting energies.

By the third day of the cruise, Joey's frustration was starting to show in small but noticeable ways. He became quieter during group activities, only speaking to me in private.

At dinner that evening, my friend made a joke—nothing malicious, but direct—and Joey's face fell. He excused himself early, leaving me and my friend at the table.

"What's his deal?" my friend asked after Joey left.

I pinched the bridge of my nose, exhaustion creeping in. "He's just… sensitive. He feels like he doesn't belong here."

"Maybe he doesn't," my friend said bluntly. "Look, I get that he's your boyfriend or whatever, but this was supposed to be your trip. I only said yes to bringing him because you asked, but now it feels like we're tiptoeing around him."

I didn't respond immediately, caught between defending Joey and acknowledging the truth in my friend's words.

Later, in our cabin, Joey was sitting on the edge of the bed, scrolling on his phone.

"You okay?" I asked, closing the door behind me.

"Why'd he have to say that?" Joey muttered, not looking up.

"Say what?"

"That joke. It was clearly aimed at me."

"It wasn't aimed at you, Joey," I said, trying to keep my tone calm. "That's just how he is. He jokes like that with everyone."

"Well, it didn't feel like a joke," Joey snapped, finally meeting my gaze. "It felt like he was trying to make me feel small."

I sat down next to him, placing a hand on his knee. "I know this trip hasn't been easy for you, and I appreciate you making the effort to come. But maybe you're reading too much into things. He doesn't know you like I do. Give him a chance."

Joey didn't respond, and the silence hung heavy between us.

The cruise was beautiful, no doubt about it. The meals were exquisite, the ports we visited were stunning, and the sunsets were unforgettable. But the tension between Joey, my friend, and even myself left a bitter aftertaste.

I realized something important during that week: Joey and I weren't as aligned as I thought. While I appreciated his excitement and effort to join me on the trip, his inability to navigate social dynamics—and my growing frustration at always playing mediator—revealed cracks in our relationship that I couldn't ignore.

This wasn't just about the cruise. It was about us, and the way we communicated—or didn't. It was a microcosm of the larger issues we'd been brushing aside.

Returning from the cruise, the weight of everything lingered like a storm cloud. Joey's insecurities were magnified, and my own frustrations, though often unspoken, began to bubble closer to the surface. I found myself walking on eggshells around him, constantly trying to navigate his moods and reassure him that he mattered.

It wasn't as though I didn't care—I did. Deeply. Joey was kind, thoughtful in his own way, and had a charm about him that made me want to protect him from the world. But protecting someone can become exhausting when you're not being protected in return.

The imbalance in our relationship was no longer subtle. It seeped into every interaction. I was always the one initiating—planning dates, solving conflicts, and trying to bridge the growing distance between us. When I brought it up to Joey, his response was always the same:

"I just don't know how to match what you do. You're so… amazing. I feel like I'll never measure up."

I would sigh, trying to tread lightly. "Joey, this isn't a competition. I'm not expecting grand gestures. I just want to feel like we're both putting in effort. Relationships shouldn't be one-sided."

He'd nod, agree to try harder, but the cycle would repeat. And every time it did, I felt more unseen.

After one particularly tense week, I brought up the idea of couples therapy. We were sitting in my apartment, the air between us thick with unspoken tension.

"Joey," I began carefully, "I think we need to talk about how we're communicating. Or… not communicating."

He looked up from his phone, his brow furrowing. "What do you mean?"

"I mean that we keep having the same conversations, the same arguments, and nothing changes. I think maybe we should see someone—together. A therapist. They can help us understand each other better."

Joey's face immediately hardened. "Therapy? You think we need therapy? Are you saying I'm crazy or something?"

"No, that's not what I'm saying at all," I replied, keeping my voice calm. "Therapy isn't about being 'crazy.' It's about learning how to communicate better, to build a stronger foundation. I'm not blaming you. I just think we could use some help."

Joey shook his head, crossing his arms. "I don't know. Therapy's not really my thing. Besides, shouldn't we be able to figure this out on our own? Isn't that what love is about?"

"Love is about effort," I countered gently. "And sometimes, that effort means asking for help. This isn't about failing, Joey. It's about trying to succeed."

He didn't respond. The conversation ended there, unresolved like so many others.

The night of the breaking point wasn't an explosive argument; it was something quieter but infinitely heavier. Joey and I were sitting in his living room, the warm glow of the table lamp the only light between us. I had just finished cleaning up after dinner—a meal I'd cooked because he'd been too tired from work—and the silence between us felt deafening.

He broke it first.

"You seem distant," Joey said, his voice soft but tinged with the familiar edge of doubt. "Do you even still love me?"

The question shouldn't have stung as much as it did. I had heard it before—too many times, in fact. But this time, it felt different, heavier, like it carried the weight of months of unresolved tension.

"Joey," I said, placing the dish towel on the counter and turning to face him, "I do love you. But I can't keep having this conversation. I've told you, shown you, done everything I can to prove how much you mean to me. What more do you need?"

He looked at me, his expression caught between sadness and frustration. "I just... I don't feel it. You say you love me, but sometimes it feels like you're pulling away."

I felt my chest tighten, the words coming faster than I could stop them. "I'm not pulling away, Joey. I'm exhausted. I'm trying so hard to keep this relationship afloat, to meet your needs, but it feels like nothing I do is ever enough."

Joey's brows furrowed, his voice raising just slightly. "Why are you making it sound like this is all my fault? Relationships are supposed to be hard sometimes!"

"Yes, they are," I agreed, taking a deep breath to steady myself. "But they're not supposed to feel impossible. They're not supposed to leave you feeling drained every single day. Joey, I'm giving everything I have, and I'm getting nothing back. It's like you expect me to pour into you endlessly without ever asking what I need in return."

His face fell, but instead of softening, he dug his heels in. "I do ask what you need," he countered, his voice trembling now. "I try to make you happy. But you're so... self-sufficient, I feel like there's nothing I can do that's good enough for you."

I shook my head, frustration mounting. "It's not about you being 'good enough.' It's about you showing up. Planning a date without me prompting you. Asking how I'm feeling without me bringing it up first. Meeting me halfway instead of waiting for me to carry all the weight."

Joey stood up, pacing the room now, his hands gesturing wildly. "So, what, you're saying I'm a bad boyfriend? That I don't care about you?"

"No, Joey," I said, my voice breaking. "I'm saying this relationship has become a one-way street. And I can't keep driving down it alone."

The argument spiraled from there, circling the same issues we'd been trying to resolve for months. Joey insisted he was doing his best, that his insecurities were just "something he couldn't control." I tried to explain that his insecurities weren't the problem—it was his refusal to work on them, to meet me in a space where we could grow together.

At one point, he sat down, burying his face in his hands. "I don't understand why you're doing this to me," he said, his voice muffled.

I crouched down in front of him, my heart breaking at the sight of his vulnerability. "Joey," I whispered, placing a hand on his knee, "this isn't something I'm doing to you. This is something I'm doing for me. For us. I've asked you to go to therapy with me. I've asked you to work on this together, to meet me halfway. But I can't do this alone anymore."

He looked up, his eyes red-rimmed. "So, that's it? You're just giving up?"

"I'm not giving up," I said, my own tears threatening to spill over. "I'm letting go. Because holding on is hurting us both more than it's helping."

The next morning, I packed up the few things I had left at his place—clothes, a toothbrush, a book I had been meaning to finish—and left without saying much. Joey didn't stop me, but his silence was louder than any argument we'd ever had.

As I drove away, I felt a profound emptiness, but also a strange sense of clarity. Joey was a good person, but we were not good for each other. And no amount of love or effort could change that.

Breaking up with Joey was the hardest decision I had made in a long time, but it was also the right one. Sometimes, love isn't about holding on—it's about knowing when to let go. For both of us, it was time to heal, to grow, and to find the balance we couldn't achieve together.

Not long after the breakup, I opted in for double jaw surgery   a long-overdue procedure I had put off for years. It felt symbolic, in a way, like I was reconstructing more than just my jaw. This was a chance to rebuild myself, to start over, and to shed the emotional weight that had been clinging to me for months.

The morning of the surgery was a blur. The sterile smell of the hospital mixed with the nervous churn in my stomach. I signed the consent forms with trembling hands, trying to focus on the fact that this was for my health and my future.

When I opened my eyes, the world was hazy. My face felt like it was on fire, swollen to the point where I barely recognized my own reflection when the nurse handed me a mirror. I was groggy, my thoughts swirling in a fog of anesthesia. But then, through the blur, I saw him. Joey.

He was sitting quietly in the corner of the room, his familiar face etched with concern.

"Hey," he whispered when he noticed I was awake.

I couldn't speak—my jaw was wired shut—but tears welled up in my eyes. I managed to raise a hand in acknowledgment, overwhelmed by the gesture.

"You're going to be okay," he said, leaning closer. "I just wanted to make sure you were all right."

Even in my groggy state, I felt the weight of his kindness. Despite everything, he was here. It was a moment of bittersweet clarity—Joey had a good heart, but his presence also reminded me of why we hadn't worked.

Later that day, something even more unexpected happened. For the first time in over a decade, my parents were in the same room together.

I hadn't seen my parents in the same room for over a decade. The tension between them had been palpable for years—each of them carrying the weight of their own resentments, their own unresolved issues. After their divorce, it felt like they had built separate lives in parallel universes, never crossing paths unless it was absolutely necessary. But here they were, standing side by side at my hospital bed, the boundaries of their past dissolving in the face of their daughter's need.

I wasn't sure how it happened—if it was because of my surgery or because they both knew I needed them—but there they were, both at my side, not as a couple, but as parents. For the first time since I was eighteen, I had both of them in my life at once.

The hospital room felt small, and yet, in that moment, it was filled with something I hadn't experienced in years: the sense of being cared for. My mother, ever the nurturer, was sitting on the side of the bed, her hand gently holding mine. My father, who had always been the silent type, was standing beside her, his large hand resting on my shoulder. I couldn't speak, but the look on their faces said everything. They were here—for me.

"How are you doing, kiddo?" My dad's voice broke the silence, low and comforting.

I couldn't answer him. My mouth was wired shut from the surgery, and even if I could have, words would have failed me. But my tear-filled eyes conveyed everything. I was overwhelmed, exhausted, and yet somehow, strangely relieved. There was a quiet healing happening within me. I couldn't explain it—maybe it was the proximity of their presence, maybe it was the realization that, despite everything, they had come together for me.

My mom's voice cracked as she spoke next, her hand tightening around mine. "We're here. We're not going anywhere, sweetheart. You don't have to be alone."

Tears filled my eyes. I wasn't sure if it was the physical pain from the surgery or the emotional release of seeing them here, together, that made me break down. But I couldn't hold it in. I had spent so many years feeling abandoned by them both in different ways, and now, here they were, both holding me.

I began to sob quietly, the tears coming faster now, as if they had been waiting for this moment to flood out of me. The kind of sobbing you do when you realize you are finally safe, even if it's just for a little while. Even if things weren't perfect, I finally felt seen. Finally, I wasn't carrying all the burdens alone.

Both of their hands gently wrapped around mine, and we sat there in silence, the only sound being my muffled sobs. There were no words to be said, no explanations needed. They had never understood the full extent of the pain I'd carried from their separation, but somehow, they knew this was what I needed now. They knew that, despite everything, I needed them together for me—for the first time since I was a child.

For a moment, I allowed myself to let go completely. I felt the weight of the years—the distance, the hurt, the loneliness—slowly start to lift, if only just a little. Maybe I couldn't heal all the wounds in one day, but this was a step. A step towards mending a family that had been broken for so long. A step towards healing myself.

When I finally quieted, my dad softly cleared his throat. "You're strong, kid. I don't need to say it. You've always been strong."

His words were like a balm to my soul. The things left unsaid between us—things that had never been resolved—felt less important in this moment. What mattered was that they were here, right now. What mattered was that they had put aside their differences to be by my side.

The room was thick with unspoken history. I could feel it in the way my parents interacted. My father's silence, his way of hovering but never quite fully engaging, spoke of years of separation. My mother's constant need to fill the space with reassurance, her overcompensating care, spoke of years of guilt. But despite the complexity of their emotions, neither of them left. And I didn't want them to.

My little sister came in shortly after, bringing a kind of lightness into the room. She was the bridge between us—always the one who could bring a laugh or lighten the mood. Her and my older sister took one look at the situation and instantly jumped into action, helping to translate for me since I could barely whisper. I could see the concern in her eyes as she looked between me and our parents. She stayed close to me, taking the night shift so that I wouldn't be alone. I felt guilty for having her take care of me, but I also felt an overwhelming sense of gratitude.

As the night dragged on, my body aching with the aftermath of surgery, I realized how much of the weight of my past had been absorbed by me. All the emotional turmoil I had carried, from my parents' divorce to my own heartbreaks, had stayed with me, making it hard to breathe. But this night—this reunion—was like a release valve, letting some of the pressure escape. I wasn't sure if I'd ever truly forgive my parents for all the years I had felt abandoned by them, but I knew that in that moment, I could accept them. I could accept us.

When I was discharged from the hospital the next day, it felt like a weight had been lifted, but only slightly. My little sister came through like a hero. She stayed with me through every moment, never leaving my side. I needed her more than I had ever realized. She assisted me in communicating with the nurses since I couldn't speak clearly yet, carefully helping me to the bathroom when I couldn't make it alone. Each time I woke her to help me, I felt a pang of guilt deep in my chest.

She never once complained, though. I could see it in her eyes, her quiet strength as she took on a role she wasn't prepared for, a role I felt I had failed at. She had always been the younger one, the one I was supposed to protect, but now, she was my caretaker.

Her presence was a comfort, but also a reminder of how much I had relied on her in a way that wasn't fair. She was my sister, not my mother. I could see the toll it was taking on her—tired eyes, a restless energy that lingered even when she was sitting quietly next to me. I wanted to tell her she could leave, to take a break, but I needed her too much to let her go.

After a few days of this, my mother stepped in. She insisted that my sister needed rest and that she would take over my care so my sister could get some sleep. I had mixed feelings. At first, I thought it was a kind gesture—a motherly instinct kicking in, maybe even the first time in a long time I saw my mother trying to fill a role that I so desperately needed. But what I didn't anticipate was how much her own struggles would cloud her ability to be the support I was hoping for.

She arrived the next morning, and for the first time since my surgery, I felt the weight of her presence in a way that unsettled me. I had been alone for a few days with my sister, and I had grown accustomed to that quiet, safe space. With my mother here, I could feel the undercurrent of her own pain—the tension that never fully went away. She was physically there, but emotionally, I could sense she was drifting in and out of her own battles.

The real trouble started that night.

I had finally drifted off into a fitful sleep, my body aching, my jaw still swollen, and the medication lulling me into a haze. Suddenly, the bedroom door slammed open, and I jolted awake, my heart racing.

There stood my mother, disheveled, her breath heavy with the stench of alcohol. I could feel the sharpness in the air, the kind of tension that comes with unspoken words. Her eyes were glassy, and her words came out in a slurred mess, cutting through the dark like a blade.

"Do you still love Joey?" she demanded, her voice sharp and insistent.

I stared at her, my chest tight with a mix of exhaustion and confusion. It was like she had just dragged me into a storm that I didn't ask for, one that I wasn't ready for. I had been so focused on surviving physically that I hadn't even begun to process the emotional chaos still raging inside me.

I tried to speak, but my voice was barely a whisper, rasping from the strain of surgery and fatigue. "Leave," I managed to croak, my body tense, a wave of anger rising inside me.

I wanted to scream at her, to tell her how hurt I was, how unfair it was that I was now battling not only the trauma of my surgery but also the emotional baggage of a fractured relationship with my own mother. But there was no energy left in me to fight. No energy left for the deep, unresolved wounds between us.

I turned my head away from her, using what little strength I had to force her out of the room. Her presence lingered for a moment, and the silence that followed was deafening. She didn't say anything else—just left, quietly. But in that moment, I realized how much of this—my healing, my recovery—wasn't just about physical scars. It was about confronting all the emotional baggage I'd been carrying for years. The burden of unspoken resentments, the pain of a relationship that had been fractured long before Joey and I had parted ways.

The next morning, I called Joey. I hated doing it—I knew it was a sign of weakness, a step backward, but I didn't know who else to turn to. My mother was in no state to help me, and my sister needed a break. Joey, despite everything, was still the one who had been there for me in the hardest moments.

When he arrived, I could tell he was conflicted—there was a mixture of concern, hesitation, and the faintest glimmer of hope in his eyes. He walked into my room cautiously, not sure how to approach me after everything that had happened.

"Are you okay?" he asked softly, his voice low.

I couldn't hold it in anymore. The dam broke the moment the door clicked shut behind him. I burst into tears, sobbing uncontrollably. It wasn't just the pain from my surgery; it was everything—the pressure, the guilt, the anger. All of it came crashing down on me. Joey sat next to me, rubbing my back silently, the weight of his presence a mix of comfort and sorrow.

Eventually, we both sat in the silence. I couldn't speak yet, but I had a way to communicate. I grabbed an expo marker and started writing on the mirror, jotting down the chaos inside me—my feelings, my frustrations, and my confusion.

We spent the next few hours like that—writing. Our goals, our dreams, our future. He wrote down everything he thought we wanted, everything he thought would bring us together again. But as we looked at the mirror, the truth became undeniable.

The writing on the wall—quite literally—spoke for itself. Joey wanted to stay where he was, rooted in his life. He wanted his father to move into the house I would buy, and he would help me with the down payment. I felt suffocated by the idea. My own dreams of independence, of moving out of state, stood in stark contrast to his.

I slowly wrote out, "Our paths aren't aligned."

Joey sighed, his shoulders slumping as he stared at the words. "I see it," he murmured, his voice low, resigned.

It was like the air had left the room. What had once been a partnership, a team, had become two people standing on opposite sides of a vast divide, both holding onto dreams that didn't fit together. And for the first time, I didn't try to convince him otherwise. I didn't apologize. I didn't beg him to understand. I just accepted it.

Two weeks later, I was finally able to drive again. I took Joey to the airport as a thank you for coming in my time of need. His trip to visit his sister was meant to be a brief escape, a way for him to recharge, but it was also the moment when everything came to a head.

Halfway to the airport, as we were driving through the quiet streets, Joey turned to me with a question I knew was coming, but I wasn't ready for.

"Are you sure we can't try again?" he asked, his voice faltering.

I gripped the steering wheel, my jaw aching with the effort. The words were difficult to say, but I knew they had to be said. "Joey," I said firmly, "we've been over this. I can't be in a relationship right now."

Silence fell between us. The tension in the car grew thick, palpable. When we reached the terminal, Joey hesitated before getting out of the car. There was a moment where I thought he might turn back, but he didn't.

"I just thought..." he trailed off, his voice cracking with the weight of everything unsaid.

I watched him in the rearview mirror as he walked into the airport. For a moment, I wondered if he'd turn around, if I'd pull back into the parking lot, and maybe we'd give it another shot. But I didn't. And neither did he.

He disappeared inside, and I drove off, the finality of it all settling heavily on my chest.

From the moment I stepped into my own life after the breakup, I was confronted with layers of pressure that I had been too afraid to see before. It wasn't just about the physical recovery from surgery. It was about understanding who I was, what I needed, and what I was willing to let go of in order to move forward.

The first lesson I had to learn was about the pressure of labels—the expectations I had internalized from society, from my family, from Joey, and from myself. I had let the idea of being in a relationship define me for so long that I had forgotten how to define myself outside of it. I thought that love was supposed to be all-encompassing, that it was supposed to be effortless. But what I discovered through this entire ordeal was that love isn't about fitting into a mold or following someone else's vision for your life. It's about knowing your own heart and trusting it enough to let go when something doesn't align.

I had lived for so long under the weight of expectations—thinking I had to be the perfect partner, the dutiful son, the brother who always had it together. But in my recovery, I realized I was suffocating under those labels. It wasn't just the weight of my surgery or the emotional turmoil from the breakout, it was the pressure of trying to be everything to everyone and losing myself in the process. I didn't owe anyone the version of myself that fit their expectations. I owed it to myself to be real, to be authentic, and to live in a way that reflected my own needs and desires.

When Joey came over, when I had to face my mother's questions, and when I finally sat down to write on that mirror, I was forced to confront the truth. Joey and I were no longer aligned, and it wasn't because we didn't care for each other—it was because we were on different paths. I had been living in a haze, unsure of what I wanted, but when I saw the words on the mirror, it was clear: I was meant to go in a different direction, one that required independence and self-discovery. And so was he.

That was the second lesson: letting go. It wasn't easy, but I had to learn to release the things that were no longer serving me—whether it was a relationship, an identity, or a way of living that no longer fit who I was becoming. Joey and I had tried, but we had reached a place where continuing to hold on would only cause more pain. Sometimes love means knowing when to walk away, not because you don't care, but because you do.

As my physical body healed, so did my spirit. I began to see that healing wasn't just about recovering from pain—it was about growing from it. I learned that healing comes when you stop fighting against the changes in your life, when you stop resisting the process of becoming the person you are meant to be. I had spent so long trying to fit into other people's narratives that I had forgotten to write my own.

And that was the final lesson: finding strength in vulnerability. It wasn't easy to face my emotions, to admit that I wasn't okay, that I needed help, that I had no clear answers. But the more I allowed myself to be vulnerable, the more I was able to connect to the truth inside me. I was allowed to be messy, uncertain, and imperfect. I didn't need to have everything figured out—I just needed to be open to the journey, to trust that I was on the right path, even when it didn't make sense.

Now, as I continue my journey, I carry those lessons with me. I know that I am enough as I am, that I don't need to prove anything to anyone, and that sometimes, the hardest thing to do is to let go of something that you once thought you couldn't live without. But in letting go, I discovered my own strength. I discovered who I am without the labels, without the expectations, and without the fear of being alone. And that is the greatest gift I could have given myself.

Reclamation

When I dropped Joey off at the airport, I thought I'd feel relief. Instead, as soon as he disappeared through the doors, tears streamed down my face. It wasn't just him I was saying goodbye to—it was the weight of everything we'd been through, the hopes we'd once shared, and the person I had been in that chapter of my life. That drive home was quiet, but in the stillness, something shifted. For the first time in a long time, I realized I was ready to move forward, to close this chapter and start writing my own story.

The weeks that followed were a blend of healing and self-reflection. I focused on my recovery, counting down the days until the wires were removed from my jaw. As those physical constraints disappeared, I began to feel the emotional burdens lifting too. I started planning—budgeting for future trips, organizing my finances, and mapping out the kind of life I wanted to build. These weren't impulsive decisions or things done to impress anyone else. This was for me.

It became clear that what I needed most was time to focus on myself. Relationships, no matter how meaningful, had always come with compromises. But this time, there was no one else to adjust for, no expectations to meet but my own. I made the choice to step away from dating and to fully invest in my own growth.

Now, at 32, I sit here reflecting on how far I've come. Sharing my journey with you feels vulnerable but also empowering. It's a reminder that the person I am today is the product of every struggle, every heartbreak, and every moment I chose to keep going.

Coming out was terrifying, but it taught me to embrace my truth. Surviving the darkest moments made me realize just how strong I am. Each twist in my story has been a lesson—some painful, some beautiful, but all meaningful.

If I've learned anything, it's that there's no perfect way to live. Life doesn't come with instructions, and growth doesn't follow a schedule. There's no universal playbook, no mold we're supposed to fit into. And that's okay. What matters is that we keep trying, that we keep showing up for ourselves.

You might feel lost at times. You might wonder if anyone understands what you're going through. But I promise, you're not alone. The road to self-discovery can be long, and it's often messy, but it's worth every step.

Stop comparing your path to others. You don't need to fit someone else's idea of success or happiness. What matters is that you define those things for yourself. If there are relationships, habits, or cycles that no longer serve you, let them go. Make space for the positivity and light that you deserve.

Take risks. Be brave. Break the cycles that hold you back. And never underestimate the power of kindness—both to others and to yourself.

As I write this, I want you to know that your story matters. It may not feel like it right now, but sharing your experiences has the power to change lives. You never know who might be inspired, comforted, or uplifted by your truth.

This is just a snippet of my journey—one filled with challenges, growth, and resilience. I'm still learning, still evolving, and still discovering who I am. And that's the beauty of it all.

So, to anyone who feels alone, misunderstood, or unsure of their place in the world: keep going. Keep believing in yourself. The darkness doesn't last forever, and there's always a light waiting to guide you through.

This is my story. And yours is still unfolding. Write it boldly.